IT ALL BEGAN WITH THE BETRAYAL.

When Susannah Goode is falsely accused of being a witch by her true love's family—the Fiers—she is burned at the stake.

Her father vows revenge, cursing Benjamin and Matthew Fier with a lifetime of unspeakable horror and bloody destruction.

Poor Mary—the daughter of Matthew Fier is the first to bear the tragedy of the fatal evil. She learns the hard way that there is no end to the curse.

Now the next generation—Ezra Fier and his children Jonathan, Abigail and Rachel—must face the Fier family curse and all the horror it brings!

Books by R. L. Stine

Available from ARCHWAY Paperbacks

THE FEAR STREET® SAGA ②
R·L·STINE

The
Secret

AN ARCHWAY PAPERBACK
Published by POCKET BOOKS
New York   London   Toronto   Sydney   Tokyo   Singapore

This book is a work of fiction. Names, characters, places and incidents are either products of the author's imagination or are used fictitiously. Any resemblance to actual events or locales or persons, living or dead, is entirely coincidental.

AN ARCHWAY PAPERBACK *Original*

 An Archway Paperback published by
POCKET BOOKS, a division of Simon & Schuster Inc.
1230 Avenue of the Americas, New York, NY 10020

ISBN: 0-671-86832-2

First Archway Paperback printing September 1993

10 9 8 7 6 5 4 3 2 1

FEAR STREET is a registered trademark of Parachute Press, Inc.

AN ARCHWAY PAPERBACK and colophon are registered trademarks of Simon & Schuster Inc.

Cover art by Bill Schmidt

Printed in the U.S.A.

IL 7+

THE FIER FAMILY TREE

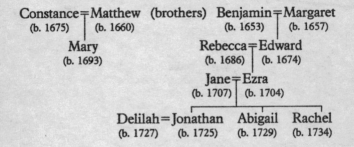

Constance═Matthew   (brothers)   Benjamin═Margaret
(b. 1675) (b. 1660)   (b. 1653) (b. 1657)

          Mary   Rebecca═Edward
        (b. 1693)   (b. 1686) (b. 1674)

                                   Jane═Ezra
                                 (b. 1707) (b. 1704)

     Delilah═Jonathan   Abigail   Rachel
    (b. 1727) (b. 1725) (b. 1729)   (b. 1734)

(100-Year Break)

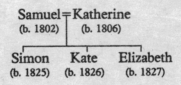

       Samuel═Katherine
      (b. 1802) (b. 1806)

    Simon   Kate   Elizabeth
  (b. 1825) (b. 1826)   (b. 1827)

The
Secret

Village of Shadyside
1900

Nora's pen scratched against the paper. Dry again. Wearily she thought of dipping the point into the inkwell, changed her mind and, yawning, set the pen down on the small writing table.

Just for a minute. Just for one minute's rest . . .

Her back ached and her fingers were cramped. She had been scribbling furiously all night by the light of a single candle.

Nora knew she had to tell her story. And she had to tell it tonight.

She touched the silver pendant that hung from a chain around her neck. Her fingers picked out the silver claws, the blue stones. Then fire appeared before her closed eyes, burning in her memory. Fire that burned the innocent Susannah Goode in 1692. Two hundred years of hatred and revenge followed Susannah's death. And then, at last, the terrible fire that consumed the Fear mansion . . .

1

Nora's eyes filled with tears. *Daniel . . . my Daniel . . .*

After so many fires, all was in ashes now.

Sighing sadly, Nora dipped her pen into the inkwell. No time to rest. The story must be told.

She heard a noise and stopped writing. She listened. Footsteps. Someone was coming!

Her hands trembling, Nora frantically shoved the paper and ink into the desk drawer. No one must see this, she thought. No one can see it until it is finished. And it is far from finished. There are so many horrors left untold.

So many horrors . . .

She held her breath, listening. The footsteps moved closer, closer . . .

PART ONE

Wickham Village, Massachusetts Colony
1737

Chapter
1

VILLAGE OF WICKHAM.

Jonathan Fier sighed with relief as the wagon rolled past the wooden sign. Their long journey was over at last.

He glanced at his father sitting beside him on the box of the wagon. Ezra Fier's face was haggard and drawn, but his black eyes sparked with excitement. He snapped the reins with renewed energy, and the chestnut horse trotted faster down the rutted, tree-lined road.

"We are here, Jonathan," Ezra said to his son. "After all those weeks in this wagon, we are finally in Wickham. George Goode is going to wish he had never been born." Ezra's voice dipped lower, almost to a whisper. "Revenge at last. It will be so sweet!"

Jonathan felt a cold chill. *Revenge*. Revenge for what?

I still do not understand, Jonathan thought. Who is George Goode? I have never even met anyone named Goode. Goodes have never done me any harm. So why did we have to leave the farm in Pennsylvania? Why have we spent the last six months driving east in this cramped and dirty old wagon?

Jonathan stole a glance at his father's gaunt face. We've come here to seek revenge against the Goodes, Papa says. Everything he does is for revenge.

Sometimes I think Papa is crazy.

Jonathan immediately wished he could take back that thought. How could I think such a thing? he scolded himself. He is my father. He cannot be crazy. There must be a reason for all the misery we have suffered. There *must* be.

"I have searched for the Goodes through five colonies," Ezra muttered. "And found no one. But now—" He paused to lift his hat and run a bony hand through his straight black hair. "Now I feel sure. I *know* they are here. I know I have found them at last."

"Ezra!" Jonathan's mother called from the back of the wagon. "Please slow down. The girls are being tossed all around!"

Ezra scowled and pulled on the reins. Jonathan turned on the box and looked back into the covered wagon.

His mother, Jane, and his two sisters, Abigail and Rachel, were huddled back there, along with all the family's possessions: pots and pans, dishes, utensils, clothes, blankets, the Fier family Bible, and the little food they had left.

"We have arrived, Mama," Jonathan said quietly. He wondered whether she would be glad or sorry.

"Hurrah!" cried three-year-old Rachel, clapping

her hands. She was a chubby angel in a homespun muslin shift with a mop of blond curls peeking out from under her cap.

Jane Fier only nodded. She was fair, with worry lines beside her clear blue eyes. She wore a printed linen dress and a loose white cap.

"I will be so happy to leave this wagon," said Abigail, a red-haired eight-year-old with mischievous blue eyes. She wore a blue- and white-striped linen dress and a white cap with blue ribbons. She looked up to her brother, Jonathan, who at almost twelve was nearly grown up. "Mama, will we be able to stop for good this time? Will we be able to sleep in a bed tonight?"

"I hope so, Abigail," Jane said.

"I will ask Papa," Abigail said.

She started for the front of the wagon, but her mother pulled her back.

"Do not bother Papa about that now," Jane whispered. "He has other matters on his mind."

He always has other matters on his mind, Jonathan thought with some bitterness. Or rather, *one* other matter.

Jonathan faced front again and lowered his black hat over his eyes. He wore his long brown hair tied back. His white linen shirt was dirty from weeks of traveling, and he was growing out of his brown homespun waistcoat and knee breeches.

As soon as we settle down, he thought, Mama will have to make me some new clothes.

No one passed them as they rolled down the leafy lane toward the village—not on horseback or on foot. It seems strangely quiet here, Jonathan thought. It is not the Sabbath. Where is everyone?

At last he saw a carriage up ahead. It was headed toward them on its way out of town.

Jonathan kept his eyes on the carriage as they approached it. It was shiny and black, a fancy carriage for rich people.

But, wait, he thought. The carriage is not moving. And where are the horses?

Something is wrong, he realized.

Something is terribly wrong.

The Fiers' wagon drew closer. Jonathan could now see two horses, but they were lying on the ground. Are they hurt? he wondered, leaning so far forward he nearly fell. Are they *dead*?

Closer.

A foul smell invaded Jonathan's nostrils. He nearly gagged.

He could see the horses clearly now. Long dead. Their flesh was rotting, their bones shoving up through the decaying skin.

"Ohhh!"

Jonathan heard his mother utter a cry of shock. He glanced back into the wagon. She had pulled his two sisters close and was covering their eyes.

Ezra slowed the wagon but did not stop.

Why was it left here on the road? Jonathan wondered. Why would people abandon such a fine carriage?

The wagon wheels creaked as they pulled close enough for Jonathon to see inside the carriage.

To his astonishment, the carriage was not empty.

Three women were inside, dressed in gowns of fine silk and white lace caps.

Jonathan stared hard at the women. Their faces.

The faces were purple, nothing but bone and chunks

of decaying flesh, poking out from beneath their fancy caps.

They're dead, Jonathan realized, covering his nose with his hand. And they've been dead a long, long time.

Rotting corpses, going nowhere in a fancy carriage.

Chapter
2

Jonathan stifled a cry and covered his face with both hands.

Why have these decaying bodies been left here? he wondered. Why have the villagers not taken them away to be buried?

Was the carriage and its rotting cargo left here as a warning?

Stay away!

Still holding his breath from the stench, Jonathan turned to gaze at his father.

Ezra was staring intently into the carriage window. Was he shocked by the figures inside? Jonathan could not tell. His father's face revealed no emotion.

"Ezra—" Jane pleaded, her voice tight and shrill. "Turn back. We cannot stay here. That carriage. Those women. I have such a bad feeling."

Ezra turned and silently glared at her in answer. She

kept her eyes leveled on him defiantly. Then, without a word, he snapped the reins and urged the horse forward. They headed into town.

Ezra guided the wagon into the village common and stopped.

Jonathan glanced around.

No sign of life. Not another person in sight.

Jonathan could hold the questions back no longer. "Papa, why are we here? Why are we searching for the Goodes? What did they do to you?"

"Jonathan, hush!" his mother cried. Her eyes were wide with fright and warning.

For a moment no one spoke. Jonathan turned from his mother back to his father. What have I done? he wondered. What will Papa do to me?

Then Ezra spoke. "He is old enough now, Jane. He is right to ask these questions. He must know the truth."

With a groan Ezra climbed down from the wagon and beckoned to his son. "Come with me, boy."

"I will come, too!" said Abigail.

Her mother pulled her back inside. "No, Abigail. You will stay here with me."

Jonathan followed Ezra across the common. He stopped short when he saw a man locked in the stocks, his head and hands thrust through the three holes in the wooden frame. His eyes were open and staring but empty. *Dead.*

Jonathan's stomach lurched. "Papa—" he managed to choke out.

But Ezra strode quickly past the wide-eyed corpse. "Our family once lived here, in Wickham," Ezra told Jonathan. "My grandfather was the magistrate.

Everyone knew him and his brother to be good and righteous men. But that very righteousness ruined their lives."

How could that be? Jonathan wondered. But he said nothing.

"Witches were discovered in Wickham. My grandfather had them burned at the stake. Two of them were Susannah and Martha Goode. They were put on trial by my grandfather, found guilty, and burned."

Now Jonathan swallowed hard. "Your grandfather —he—he burned people at the stake?"

"Not people—*witches!*" Ezra boomed. "Vile and evil creatures of the devil!" Ezra paused, breathing hard. "My grandfather and his brother did their duty."

Jonathan shuddered at the thought of women being burned alive. But he said nothing.

"Our family moved from Wickham to Pennsylvania," Ezra continued, calmer now. "But William Goode, the father of Susannah, the husband of Martha, followed them. He believed his wife and daughter to be innocent. Driven by revenge, William used dark powers against my grandfather and his family.

"William disguised himself as a young man. He took advantage of my aunt Mary's innocence and—" Ezra paused again, searching for words.

"And what, Papa?"

"William Goode destroyed our family. He killed my grandfather and my mother. The rest he drove insane. I found my great-uncle and his wife buried behind a brick wall—nothing left of them but bones."

Jonathan gasped. *This* was his family history! And it was the reason behind his father's obsession. It explained why his father hated the Goodes with such passion.

Still, something did not make sense to Jonathan. In his almost twelve years, Jonathan had never seen a sign of this William Goode or his black magic.

No member of the Goode family had ever appeared during Jonathan's life to seek revenge against the Fiers. So why was Ezra keeping the evil feud alive? Why was Ezra determined to spend his life searching for Goodes?

"Papa," Jonathan asked hesitantly, "is William Goode still alive?"

"I do not know," Ezra replied bitterly. "He would be very old. I do know he had a son, George. George lived in Wickham once. I am hoping—"

He did not finish the sentence, but Jonathan knew what he was hoping. He hoped to find this George Goode, or other Goodes, and bring them misery.

And that is why we have come to Wickham, Jonathan realized.

But so far we have not seen a living soul. Only corpses.

This town *must* be cursed.

"Come," Ezra said. "We will go to the tavern and ask after the Goodes." Ezra led Jonathan up the tavern steps.

The innkeeper will tell us what has happened, Jonathan thought. Innkeepers always know the news.

Ezra opened the tavern door. They stepped inside.

The room was empty. The fireplace stood cold and dark, the tables covered with dust and cobwebs. Plates of food had rotted on one of the tables. It may have been a meal of roast lamb and a pudding. Rats scurried around the table, gnawing at the mold-covered meal.

Ezra grunted unhappily, his features set in disappointment. Jonathan saw a pile of dust-covered letters on the bar, probably left there for the villagers to pick up. The letters had been delivered a long time ago.

The floorboards creaked under Ezra's boots as he walked over to the bar to sort through the letters. About halfway through the pile, he stopped. He rubbed the dust from the front of the envelope and carefully studied the address.

"Papa?" said Jonathan.

Ezra looked up at his son. "Go find the village magistrate's house," he ordered. "Ask if the magistrate will see me. I will be along in a minute."

"Yes, sir," Jonathan replied meekly and walked quickly from the tavern. Outside he hesitated.

Where could he find the magistrate? The street was empty. There was no one to ask.

Then he spotted a large house on the other side of the common. It was the grandest house in the village, sided with clapboards weathered brown, and enclosed by an unpainted picket fence. It stood two stories tall, with glass windows and two chimneys.

This *must* be the magistrate's house, Jonathan told himself, making his way across the common, half-walking, half-running. It felt good to run after his long journey.

Jonathan lifted the heavy brass door knocker and let it drop. No answer. How strange that such a fine house should have a broken parlor window, he thought.

He cupped his hand around his eyes and peered

through the window beside the door. The parlor was dark.

He turned the doorknob and uttered a soft cry of surprise when the door opened easily at his touch.

"Hello?" he called. His voice echoed through the house.

Jonathan quietly stepped inside. "Hello?" he repeated in a trembling voice. "I am here to see the magistrate."

The house remained silent. Jonathan made his way into the parlor. The heavy thud of his boots on the floorboards was the only sound. "Hello?"

No one was in the parlor, which led to a smaller room. Some kind of office, perhaps? "Hello? Is the magistrate at home?" Jonathan stepped into this second doorway.

Squinting into the dim light, Jonathan saw an old man at a desk with his back to the door. Jonathan could make out long gray hair falling onto the collar of a brown coat.

Jonathan knocked lightly on the frame of the open door and said, "Sir? May I come in? Sir?"

The old man did not move.

Jonathan took a deep breath and stepped into the room. He made his way up to the high-backed chair and gently tapped on the man's shoulder. "Sir? Sir?"

The man moved—and Jonathan started to scream.

Chapter
3

Jonathan's scream echoed off the walls of the tiny room.

The man toppled and slid to the floor.

Panting loudly, struggling to keep from screaming again, Jonathan gazed wide-eyed at the hideous face.

The man's long gray hair rested on nothing but bone. The grinning skull stared up at Jonathan, its teeth yellow and rotting. As Jonathan gaped down, frozen in horror, a spider crawled out from the deep, empty eye socket.

Jonathan shrieked out his horror. He wanted to run, but his feet seemed to be nailed to the floor. He couldn't take his eyes from the white-haired, grinning skeleton.

He screamed again.

"Jonathan! Jonathan! What is wrong?" Ezra shouted, bursting into the room. Ezra stopped and stared down at the corpse. "Come. We must go," he said softly. Placing his hands on Jonathan's shoulders, he guided the boy from the room.

Outside, Ezra ordered, "Go back to the wagon and sit with your mother and sisters. I will be there soon. Just stay put and wait for me."

"Yes, Papa," said Jonathan, grateful to be out in the fresh air. He walked slowly back to the wagon, breathing deeply, trying to slow his racing heart.

He didn't want to scare his mother. But he knew she would ask him what he had seen. And there was no way to describe it without frightening her. No way to say it that wouldn't be horrible to hear.

No one lived in the town of Wickham, Jonathan realized as a wave of terror swept over him.

Every single human had died.

Wickham was dead, a town of rotting corpses.

"What have you found?" his mother asked eagerly as Jonathan stepped up to the wagon. "Where is your father?"

"Papa will be back soon," said Jonathan. "He is exploring the village."

"Did you talk to the innkeeper?" Jane demanded. "Why was that carriage left on the road? Did he say anything?"

"No, Mama," said Jonathan softly. "There was no innkeeper. There is . . . no one."

Jane leaned forward, her eyes burning into his. She chewed her lower lip. "Jonathan, what do you mean?"

"Everyone is dead," said Jonathan. "Everyone. There is no one left alive in the whole town."

Jane gasped. She started to say something, but Ezra

17

returned. He climbed up beside Jonathan on the box and, without saying a word, cracked the reins. The wagon lurched forward with a jolt.

"Ezra?" cried Jane. "What is it? Where is everyone? What did you find out?"

"Plague," Ezra answered flatly, narrowing his eyes and staring straight ahead. "No survivors."

"And the Goodes?"

"We shall soon see," Ezra said.

Ezra drove the wagon out of town, the wooden wheels bouncing over the rutted dirt road. He said nothing. His expression remained set, hard and thoughtful.

He didn't slow the horses until they came to a farmhouse. It was a wooden saltbox house, smaller than the magistrate's, but still two stories tall with a small attic. A brick chimney ran through the middle of the house. A shed connected the kitchen to a big barn.

Ezra pulled the wagon up to the door of the house and stopped the horse.

Is this the Goodes' house? Jonathan wondered. Will they be dead, too? Will they be alive?

Ezra lowered himself to the ground and made his way to the door. He knocked. Three solid knocks.

And waited.

No answer.

Jonathan watched his father open the door and step inside. "Jonathan," Jane whispered, giving him a shove. "Go with him."

Jonathan climbed down from the wagon. Abigail slipped out, too, before her mother could stop her. They followed Ezra into the farmhouse.

Stepping into the front parlor, Jonathan's eyes

explored the room. He was somewhat surprised to find it neat and tidy. He saw no sign of anyone, dead or alive. It felt as if the people who lived there had left.

"Hello?" he called. But he was not surprised when he received no answer.

"They must be here!" Ezra exclaimed with emotion. "They *must!* I will not rest until I see their rotting corpses with my own eyes."

Ezra ran up the stairs. Standing in the parlor with his sister, Jonathan could hear his father's frantic footsteps above him.

Ezra ran from room to room. Jonathan then heard Ezra climb up to the attic. When Ezra returned, he ran past the children as if not seeing them. Jonathan heard him as he explored the large common room, the shed, and the barn.

A few minutes later Ezra returned to the parlor, his face purple with rage.

"Papa, what *is* it?" Jonathan cried.

Chapter
4

"They are gone!" Ezra screamed. "A plague has killed everyone in Wickham—*but the Goodes have escaped!*"

Jane Fier ran into the house with Rachel in her arms. "Please, Ezra," she pleaded, tugging at her husband's sleeve. "We must leave this horrible place. The Goodes are not here. We must leave!"

Ezra shook her off. "No," he replied firmly. "We will stay here, Jane. The Goodes lived here not long ago. Somewhere in this house there will be a clue to tell us where they have gone."

He made his way to a desk in the corner and started digging through the drawers.

Jane followed him, weeping. "Ezra, we cannot stay here! We cannot! We cannot stay here all alone with only corpses for neighbors!"

"Wife—" Ezra started.

"Think of your children!" Jane cried, holding the baby against her chest.

"Silence!" Ezra screamed, pushing her away. He glared furiously at her. Jonathan trembled when he saw that mad gleam in his father's eyes.

"I have heard enough from you, Jane!" Ezra cried sternly. "No more pleading and no more questions! From now on I expect obedience from all of you—obedience and nothing else!"

No one moved. Abigail whimpered softly. Ezra's harsh expression didn't soften.

"I am going to find the Goodes," he said slowly through gritted teeth. "They cannot escape me. I am going to find them. *And nothing will stop me!*"

Jonathan's mother ran from the room, crying. Abigail clung to Jonathan's side, and he put an arm around her tiny shoulders.

Ezra said, "Jonathan, start unpacking the wagon. This house will be our new home."

Jonathan gasped. We are going to live *here,* in someone else's house? he wondered, horrified by the idea. We are going to live here, so near the frightening village of corpses?

"Jonathan—do as you are told!" ordered his father, his voice booming through the house.

"Yes, Papa," Jonathan said.

With a sinking heart, Jonathan hurried outside. His hands trembling, he unhitched the horse and led him into the barn.

We are going to live in their house, he thought. The Goodes' own house, with all their things in it. What if they are not dead? What if they come back—and find us here?

21

He found a bucket in the barn and carried it outside. There was a pump in the yard. He pumped water into the bucket and took it to the horse.

At least we will have a place to sleep tonight, he told himself. With a featherbed. And a hearth to cook by.

Jonathan sighed. Maybe it will not be so bad here, he thought. He gazed around at the green fields, the apple orchard in the distance, and the cozy house. Smoke was already rising from the chimney. His mother must have started a fire.

Maybe we will be happy here, he thought. If only the Goodes do not come back. . . .

The Fiers found everything they needed in the Goodes' house. Jonathan discovered preserves, smoked meat, and cornmeal in the shed. Abigail found a bolt of linen in the attic. Soon she and Jonathan had fresh new clothes made from the linen.

Their mother kept busy cooking, cleaning, spinning, and sewing. Abigail helped her mother and took care of Rachel. Jonathan did the heavy chores: chopping wood, drawing water, caring for the horse. When his mother was very busy, he also looked after the girls for her.

As they all settled in to their new life, Jonathan's only concern was for his father. Ezra Fier had only one thing on his mind—where had the Goodes gone?

Jonathan watched his father rummage through storage bins and drawers reading every scrap of paper he could find, studying anything that might give him a clue to their whereabouts.

He thinks of nothing but revenge, Jonathan thought angrily, watching his father read ledgers one day. He wouldn't even eat if Mama didn't put a plate of food in front of him every evening. Nothing distracts him from the Goodes.

Then Abigail ran into the room, shouting, "Papa! Look at me!"

Ezra glanced up from the ledger, and Jonathan saw his father's scowl melt into a smile. "Where did you get that pretty dress?" Ezra asked. "Turn around for me."

Abigail tossed a lock of red hair off her forehead and turned slowly, showing off her new blue dress.

"Mama found it in the back of an old wardrobe upstairs," she explained, her blue eyes twinkling. "It fits me perfectly!"

Ezra held his arms out, and Abigail ran to him for a hug. Releasing her, he said, "Run along now and help your mama. I have work to do here."

"Yes, Papa," Abigail said. She skipped out of the room.

Papa looks almost happy, Jonathan thought as he watched his father. Abigail is the only one who can do that. She is the only one who can still make Papa smile.

Quickly Ezra's smile faded, and he turned to Jonathan and demanded, "What are you looking at, boy? You have chores to do, have you not?"

"Yes, Papa," said Jonathan. He hurried out of the room.

About three weeks after they had moved into the house, Ezra called Jonathan to him. "Hitch up the wagon," Ezra said. "We are going to call on our neighbors."

There were a couple of farmhouses a few miles down the road. Jonathan knew that people were living in them because he could see smoke rising from that direction every morning.

The Fiers' wagon stopped in front of a large, prosperous-looking farmhouse with red chickens pecking around the yard. Jonathan saw a young woman working in the garden, bending low to pull out weeds. She stood up when she saw Jonathan and Ezra approach.

Ezra took off his hat. "Good day, miss," he said. "Is the master of the house at home?"

The young woman curtsied and hurried excitedly into the house, calling, "Papa! We have visitors!"

A gray-haired man with a big belly topping tooth-pick legs came out of the front door and introduced himself in a friendly way. Ezra removed his hat to introduce himself and Jonathan.

"We have just moved into the area, Master Martin," Ezra explained. "We are looking for a family named Goode."

At the mention of the name Goode, the older man blinked hard. His face turned pale.

"We thought the Goodes were living down the road, but they are gone," Ezra continued. "Would you happen to know what has become of them?"

The man's friendly expression faded, replaced by a scowl. "I do not know the Goodes," he said gruffly. "I am sorry. I cannot help you. Good day, Master Fier."

Abruptly the man hurried back into his house, shutting the door behind him and his daughter. Jonathan saw the girl's face at the window. The old man pulled her away.

Ezra began to shake with rage. "What can this mean?" he cried. "Why does he refuse to speak to us?"

"Perhaps they know something at the next farm, Papa," Jonathan said softly, trying to calm his father.

They continued on to the next farm, three miles away. This one appeared poorer, a smaller house with rocky fields behind it. A thin old man tilled the field with a single hoe.

"Good day, sir," called Ezra, tipping his hat as he approached. "May I have a word with you?"

The man stopped but made no move toward them. He stared at Jonathan and Ezra suspiciously.

"What is it, then?" he asked in a surly voice.

"My name is Ezra Fier," Ezra told him. "This is my son, Jonathan. We are looking for a family in the region and wondered if you knew what had become of them."

"What family is that?" asked the old man, leaning on the hoe now.

Ezra cleared his throat. "The family of George Goode," he said.

The man's scowl deepened. He remained still for a moment, leaning on the hoe, his eyes studying Ezra. Then he raised himself, turned, and strode quickly toward his barn.

Ezra nodded at Jonathan. "He is going to tell us something," he whispered. They followed the old man across the rocky ground to his barn.

The old man disappeared inside. Jonathan and Ezra waited several yards from the door.

In a moment the man came running out, holding a long knife.

Ezra smiled uncertainly. Then Jonathan saw the confusion on his face.

Before Ezra could move, the man had pressed the knife to Ezra's neck. "I am going to cut your throat," he snarled.

Chapter
5

Ezra's body stiffened.

With a low grunt the man tightened his grip and held the knife blade tight against Ezra's skin.

"Stop—please!" cried Jonathan. "We have done nothing wrong!"

"George Goode was the child of a witch!" said the man. "His evil brought the plague to our village—and he escaped it! What do *you* want with George Goode?"

"We are no friends of his, believe me," Ezra choked out. "We wish him nothing but harm."

The man relaxed a little, easing the knife blade back a few inches from Ezra's throat. "Get off my farm," he growled. "Do not come back, ever. And never dare to ask about the villainous Goodes again."

He released Ezra. Ezra and Jonathan hurried to the wagon and drove off.

"Remember this day, son," Ezra said solemnly. "This is further proof of the evil of the Goodes. We are not the only people they have harmed."

The next day Jonathan's father went back to searching the house. "I must have missed something," Jonathan heard him muttering. "What are they hiding? What are they hiding?"

Jonathan carried a stack of firewood inside one morning as his mother sat sewing by the hearth with Rachel on her lap. Abigail stood over a basin full of water, scrubbing the last of the breakfast dishes.

"Mama says I have no more chores to do today," Abigail said happily. "Not until suppertime. I am going to go exploring."

"Watch her, Jonathan, please," said his mother. "Do not let her stray too far."

Abigail tossed the dirty dishwater out the door and wiped her hands on her apron. She pulled on her cap and ran outside, the blue ribbons on her cap flying.

Jonathan followed her. "Shall we go to the creek?" he suggested.

"I have already been to the creek," said Abigail. "I want to go into the village."

Jonathan stopped. "Into Wickham? But why, Abby? There is nobody there."

"I know," said Abigail. "We can go anywhere we like. There is no one to stop us!"

"No," said Jonathan. "Mama said you should not stray too far. The village is too far."

"Are you scared, Jonathan?"

Jonathan bristled. Was his younger sister daring him? "Nothing scares me," he said, although he knew that was not true. His father scared him, for one. And all those dead people in the village . . .

"Come on," said Abigail. "I am going to the village. If you must keep an eye on me, then you will just have to come along."

She ran down the road with Jonathan following close. He felt nervous about going back to the village, but he could not let his younger sister go alone.

The streets were as quiet and empty as before. The silence roared in Jonathan's ears. He heard no dogs barking, no birds chirping, no insect sounds.

"What do you think they were like?" Abigail whispered. "The people who lived here?"

"I do not know," said Jonathan. "Like us, I suppose."

They walked down the dirt road to the village common. Abigail found a small pile of bones lying under a tree.

"Look, Jonathan," she said sadly. "This was a puppy."

Jonathan stared at the grisly little skeleton. Maybe we should not be here, he thought. He glanced around. Were all the people in the town really dead?

"The poor puppy should not have to lie in the sun like this," said Abigail. "I think we should bury him."

"We have no shovel," said Jonathan.

"We can get one," Abigail said, indicating the houses and sheds all around them. "I am sure any one of these sheds will have a shovel in it."

"We cannot just take somebody's shovel, Abby," Jonathan said.

"Why not?" Abigail demanded. "It is not stealing. They are dead."

Yes, Jonathan thought. They are dead. And their bodies are still sitting inside these houses, just as this puppy's bones are lying out here in the sun.

Jonathan shuddered. He did not want Abigail to go into one of the houses to find a dead person.

"I will get a shovel," he said. "You wait here."

He walked up to the nearest house—maybe the house where the puppy had lived, Jonathan thought. It was a little wooden cottage, only two rooms.

Abigail stood right behind him as he gingerly pushed open the door.

"I told you to stay by the tree," Jonathan said gruffly.

"I want to come with you," she said. "I am too scared to be alone."

Jonathan sighed and took her hand.

It was dark inside the cottage. Jonathan's eyes took a moment to adjust to the darkness.

Abigail clutched Jonathan's sleeve. They stood frozen in the doorway.

Then Abigail whispered, "Go get the shovel."

Jonathan stepped carefully across the room. He opened a cupboard beside the back door of the cottage.

Inside the cupboard, something gleamed white with two dark and empty eye sockets glaring out.

A skeleton.

Jonathan leapt back. Abigail screamed.

The skeleton shifted. It toppled out of the closet and clattered to the floor.

Jonathan leaned over it, panting, trying to slow the frantic beating of his heart.

Then he started backing away.

"Wait!" Abigail whispered. "I see a shovel in the cupboard."

Jonathan forced himself to glance back into the cupboard. He saw the shovel. But he did not want to get it.

"Get it!" demanded Abigail. She gave him a shove.

He stepped carefully around the clutter of bones on the floor—all that remained of the skeleton. Then, holding his breath, he snatched the shovel and ran out of the house.

He was glad to be back outside in the bright sunlight. He followed Abigail to the tree and dug a little hole. Then he laid the puppy's bones in the grave. Abigail stood beside him with a branch in her hand.

"Dominatio per malum," she chanted solemnly, waving the branch over the puppy's grave.

"What does that mean?" Jonathan asked.

"I do not know," said Abigail. "Those are the words on that sparkly thing Papa wears around his neck."

Jonathan knew the words, too. The silver pendant with four blue stones had always fascinated him. He had once asked his father what the words meant, but Ezra refused to tell him.

Squinting against the bright sunlight, Jonathan covered the bones with dirt. Then Abigail planted the branch in the ground as a marker.

They were late for supper that evening. Ezra was already seated at the table with his usual preoccupied expression. Jonathan entered the kitchen first, and Ezra barked at him, "Where have you been?"

"Outside" was all Jonathan said.

Abigail came in next, and Ezra smiled. She went to

him and gave him a kiss. He played with the blue ribbons on her cap.

"You are keeping an eye on your sister, I hope," Ezra said to Jonathan.

"Yes, Papa," Jonathan replied quietly. He revealed nothing about going into the village. He knew it would make his father angry. Abigail kept it a secret, too.

A few days later Jonathan saw Abigail skipping past the barn, heading for the road. Alarmed, he chased after her. "Where are you going?" he called.

"To the village," she replied without stopping.

He took her hand and pulled her to a stop. "You cannot go," he said sternly. "I am supposed to be watching you."

"You can watch me in the village," she replied impatiently.

Jonathan sighed and followed after her.

That day they found the skeletons of two small animals—possibly a cat and a chipmunk. Abigail insisted on burying them, too.

"I am going to come back as often as I can," she told her brother as she stuck a branch in the ground by the tiny graves. "I will find all the poor dead animals and bury them all."

The next time Abigail set out for the village, Jonathan didn't try to stop her. He knew it was useless. He was getting used to the village and all its death, and didn't even mind the awful silence so much anymore.

Then one day, when they were playing in Wickham, Abigail came across the remains of a little girl. The skeleton wore a rotting blue dress that once must have been pretty, and a cap like Abigail's.

"I think we should bury her," said Abigail. "She deserves a proper funeral as much as an animal does."

"We will need a coffin," Jonathan said. "We cannot bury a person in the dirt like a dog or a cat."

"Yes," agreed Abigail. "You go find a box, and I will look for a place to bury her."

Jonathan crossed the village common and entered the tavern to search for a girl-size box. He found a wooden crate. It was a little short, but it would have to do.

He hoisted the crate onto his shoulder and carried it outside to Abigail. He didn't see her by the meeting-house where he had left her.

"Abigail?" he called, immediately worried.

No answer.

After setting the crate on the ground, he walked down the road. He heard high-pitched giggling behind the village magistrate's house.

Jonathan peered around the side of the house. He uttered a low cry of surprise when he spotted Abigail. She was playing with another little girl!

Jonathan stared at the little girl, startled to see another living person in Wickham. She was skinny, with long blond curls poking out from under her cap, and gray eyes. Where on earth had she come from? he wondered.

He started toward his sister. "Abigail—" he began.

At the sight of him, the other little girl darted behind a tree.

"You frightened her, Jonathan!" Abigail scolded. "No need to worry, Hester," she called to her friend. "It is only my brother."

But the little girl did not come out from behind the

tree. "She must be afraid of boys," Abigail said. She hurried behind the tree to look for the girl.

A second later Abigail reappeared, bewildered. "She is gone!" she told her brother. "She disappeared! And we were having so much fun together."

"Abby—who is she?" asked Jonathan.

"She told me her name is Hester," Abigail answered. "She is very nice."

"Where does she live?"

Abigail shrugged. "She did not say. But I hope she comes back. It was so pleasant to have someone to play with."

Jonathan wondered who this playmate could possibly be. Did she live in Wickham? Could there still be living people in the village?

What a mystery!

The next day, as Jonathan was digging a grave for a baby, Abigail had wandered off to find a stick for a marker. When Jonathan finished digging the hole, Abigail still had not returned.

She may be playing with her friend again, Jonathan thought. I think I will watch them for a few minutes and see what I can learn about that strange girl.

He crept over to the big house, but the girls were not there. He found them playing in the graveyard.

Ducking behind a grave slab, he leaned against the cold stone and spied on them.

Hester twirled around and laughed. She has a pretty, bell-like laugh, Jonathan thought. Just then Hester took Abigail's hand, and the two girls wove a path through the gravestones.

Hester stopped before a hole in the ground. She reached down to tug at something in the hole. Up came the lid of a coffin.

THE SECRET

Jonathan stood frozen, watching.

Hester stepped into the coffin and reached up for Abigail's hand.

Abigail touched Hester's hand.

With a firm jerk, Hester pulled Abigail into the coffin.

Chapter
6

—————————

"Abigail—no!" Jonathan shouted. He burst from his hiding place and ran to the grave.

I must get her out of there! he thought, his heart pounding. I must save her.

He stopped at the edge of the hole, stared down, and—

Abigail popped up out of the coffin, laughing.

Furious, Jonathan grabbed her arms and yanked his little sister out of the coffin. "Stop playing foolish games," he scolded angrily. "We have to go home now."

"But, Jonathan, Hester and I—"

Refusing to listen to her protests, he pulled her along behind him.

We must get away from here, he thought, forgetting the other girl.

Abigail dragged her feet and glanced back at Hester.

"Why do we have to go home?" she asked. "I was having fun."

"We just do." Jonathan didn't want to admit the truth—he was afraid.

Afraid of what? Of a little girl?

He did not know. But he knew that something was not right.

"Jonathan, you and Abby must stay in today," his mother said. "I need you both to watch Rachel for me."

Abigail groaned. "I wish we could go back to the village," she whispered to Jonathan. "I was looking forward to playing with Hester."

But Jonathan was secretly relieved. He said nothing about it to Abigail, but he was determined not to go to Wickham anymore.

Hester pulled Abby into an open coffin, he remembered with a shudder. I must keep Abby away from her.

Jonathan and Abigail were playing with Rachel in front of the hearth, rolling a ball along the floor to her, when Ezra appeared.

"Hello, Papa," said Abigail brightly.

Ezra flashed her a smile. "Would you like to go for a walk with me? I need a bit of air."

"Mama asked me to watch Rachel today," Abigail told him.

"Jonathan can watch Rachel," said Ezra. "Come along with me. I like your company."

Abigail jumped up and went outside with her father. Feeling a little hurt, Jonathan watched them through the window.

He gasped when he saw her.

Hester.

Jonathan saw her run up to Abigail and Ezra. Curious, Jonathan picked up Rachel and hurried outside to see what would happen.

He could see the surprise on his father's face as Abigail introduced Hester to him.

"Where do you live, Hester?" Ezra asked.

"Nearby," Hester replied shyly.

"And who are your parents?" Ezra demanded.

"Mama and Papa," answered the blond little girl.

Ezra pointed in the direction of the farmhouses a few miles down the road. "So you live there?"

"She is a good girl, Papa," Abigail interrupted, her eyes shining. She was clearly happy to have a playmate.

Hester turned her sparkling gray eyes on Ezra and asked, "Can Abigail come to my house?"

Abigail tugged at his sleeve. "Please, Papa," she begged. "Please?"

Jonathan stepped forward. "Do not let her go, Papa," he said.

Ezra turned sharply to his son. "Why not?"

Jonathan glanced uneasily at Hester and Abigail. "I cannot say, Papa. I just know you must not let her go."

"Please let me go with Hester," Abigail said. "It is so good to have a friend." Tears were forming in her eyes.

Ezra gazed lovingly at his daughter. Jonathan knew his father could deny Abigail nothing. He knew what would happen next.

"All right, Abigail. You may go."

"Papa," urged Jonathan, "let me go with her."

"No," Ezra said firmly. "You will stay here. Someone must watch the baby."

"But, Papa——"

"You heard me, Jonathan," Ezra said, his temper rising. "You are too old to play with little girls. You will stay here."

He turned to Abigail and added, "Run along, but be home for supper."

"I will!" Abigail called back happily. She ran off with Hester, the blue ribbons on her cap flying behind her.

Jonathan stared after his sister, watching her until they disappeared over the hill.

"Jonathan, your mother is calling you," said Ezra. "Do you not hear?"

"Yes, Papa," said Jonathan. He carried Rachel inside to his mother.

The sun had gone down, and Abigail had not returned home.

"Supper is ready, Jonathan," his mother said. "I will take Rachel now."

She picked up the baby and put her into the wooden high chair. Jonathan took his place at the table, gazing at the darkening sky beyond the window.

Supper, and still Abby is not home, he thought anxiously.

His mother took a pot of chicken stew off the fire and called Ezra to the kitchen. Jonathan could see that his father was worried, too. Deep lines furrowed Ezra's brow, and his eyes were dark and troubled. But Jonathan did not dare say a word.

Jane Fier went to the door and called, "Abigail! Supper!"

There was no response.

"Where is that girl?" Jane wondered aloud.

"She went off to play with a friend," Ezra said quietly. "I expect she will be back soon."

"A friend?" said Jane. "What friend?"

"A little girl," Ezra answered. He looked uncomfortable. "A sweet girl. She lives nearby."

Jane glanced at Jonathan. He knew she wanted him to explain to her, but he said nothing. He knew his mother was frightened, too, but she tried to hide it. "The stew is getting cold," she said stiffly. "We shall have to start without her."

She dished out the chicken stew. The family began to eat. No one spoke.

Beyond the window the sky darkened. Still no sign of Abigail.

Jonathan glanced up, and his mother met his eyes. He turned to Ezra, who was carefully cutting the bits of chicken into smaller and smaller pieces, but not eating a single one.

Jane Fier suddenly stood up. "Ezra, I am worried," she said. "What could be keeping her?"

Ezra stared out at the black sky. He wiped his mouth with his napkin and stood up.

"I am going to look for her," he said.

"Let me go with you, Papa," Jonathan asked.

"No!" Ezra snapped. "Stay with your mother and sister."

He threw on his hat. Then he took the lamp from its hook by the fireplace, lit it with a twig, and walked out into the darkness.

I must go with him, Jonathan thought desperately. He does not know where to search. Only I do.

He decided to follow Ezra.

"I do not want to leave you alone, Mama," he said. "But Papa needs my help."

Jane nodded and said, "Go with him."

Jonathan slipped outside, following a few paces behind the glow of his father's lantern. The evening sky was purple, growing darker every second. A crescent moon hovered over the horizon.

"Abigail!" Ezra called. "Abigail!" He began to walk down the road toward the other farmhouses, away from Wickham.

He is going the wrong way, Jonathan thought in frustration. But then he saw his father stop and stand still, as if he were listening to something. Jonathan listened, too.

There was a soft, sweet sound. Laughter. A little girl's laughter.

Where was it coming from?

Ezra turned in confused circles. The laughter seemed to float on the air from all directions at once.

The voice giggled again. Now it sounded as if it came from the village.

Ezra walked toward it, following the sound.

Jonathan trailed his father into the village. He had never seen it at night before. It felt emptier than ever. Ezra's lantern cast eerie shadows on the trees and houses. The shadows made the houses seem to move and breathe.

"Abigail!" Ezra called again, then stopped and listened.

The little laugh chimed on the wind.

"Is that you, Abigail?" Ezra called out. "Where are you?"

The laugh came again, a little louder, like the tinkling of sleigh bells.

41

That is not Abigail, Jonathan thought. His father seemed to realize it, too.

"Who are you?" Ezra cried. "Show yourself to me!"

The only response was another girlish giggle. Ezra moved toward it, with Jonathan right behind him.

Staying far enough behind not to be seen, Jonathan followed his father to the graveyard. Ezra stumbled among the crooked gravestones, the little laugh teasing him, taunting him, leading him farther into the maze of headstones.

The lantern flashed a ghoulish yellow light on the gray markers. "Abigail!" Ezra cried, his voice cracking now. "Please come out!"

Ezra stopped again to listen, but this time there was no laughter.

Jonathan crept up closer and stood right behind his father. Ezra did not notice.

Ezra was standing at the foot of a grave. He held the lantern out so it illuminated the name on the marker.

It read, "Hester Goode."

Jonathan could hear Ezra gasp.

Goode? Did the marker really say "Hester *Goode?*"

Then a light breeze blew, and on the breeze came the sound of a voice.

Not laughter this time, but words. Words spoken in the same girlish voice that had led them to this spot.

"Can Abigail come to my house?"

Hester!

Hester's grave. Hester was not living, Jonathan realized to his horror.

Hester was dead.

But still she called.

"Can Abigail come to my house?"

Still she called. Called from the grave.

42

Abby's little playmate, giggling and calling from the grave.

"Can Abigail come to my house?"

Slowly Ezra moved the lantern to the right.

His hand trembled. He nearly dropped the lantern as it cast its light on another grave.

Freshly dug.

With a new headstone.

The light fell across the inscription on the gray stone.

It read: *"Abigail Fier."*

"No!" Ezra tossed back his head and howled.

The lantern slid from his hand and rolled into the dirt.

Ezra dropped to his knees, still howling. "Abigail! Abigail!" he cried over and over, clawing at the dirt, trying to dig her up.

Shuddering in terror, Jonathan bent over his father, reached for his father's heaving shoulders, tried to stop his father's mournful cries.

Ezra pushed him roughly away.

The breeze blew again, and with it came the laughter. And the taunting request: *"Can Abigail come to my house?"*

Uttering animal cries, Ezra tore at the dirt with his fingers. Desperate, Jonathan began to dig, too. Ezra made no move to stop him now.

It was a shallow grave. Jonathan's fingers soon touched the smooth, polished wood of a coffin.

"No!" Ezra shrieked. "No! Please—No!" With a grunt he shoved Jonathan out of the way and tore open the lid of the coffin.

There lay little Abigail, her eyes closed, her lips white, her face a pale, bluish mask.

She was dead.

"Curse them! Curse them!" Ezra screamed. "The Goodes will pay! They will burn again!"

Then his expression changed. The hatred melted into grief and horror. He lowered his face to his hands, sobbing, "Abigail, Abigail."

Jonathan choked back his own tears and helped his weeping father to his feet. Holding each other and sobbing, they stood motionless in the silent darkness.

Hester Goode's gleeful laughter surrounded them, ringing in their ears.

No matter how they tried, they couldn't stop her gleeful chant:

"Abigail came to my house! Abigail came to my house!"

PART TWO

Western Massachusetts
1743

Chapter
7

"And ever since that day, our family has been cursed. The Goodes will not let us live in peace. That is why we must find them and put an end to this horror, once and for all."

Jonathan Fier stopped outside his sister Rachel's bedroom door to listen. Their father, Ezra, was putting Rachel to bed.

Every night Ezra told his daughter a bedtime story. But instead of reciting a fairy tale, Ezra told her the story of the family curse.

Some bedtime story, Jonathan thought sadly. I am surprised it does not give her nightmares.

"I do not want to go to sleep, Papa," Rachel said. "Please, let me stay up a little longer. It is still light out."

"No," Ezra replied firmly. "Get into bed and stay there this time. I mean it."

47

Jonathan smiled as he heard this. Rachel always hated to go to bed before everyone else.

"But Jonathan does not have to go to bed," she whined.

"Jonathan is almost eighteen and you are a little nine-year-old girl," said Ezra. "I do not want to hear any more about it. Shut your eyes. Good night."

Jonathan hurried down the hall before Ezra came out of Rachel's room. He did not want his father to catch him eavesdropping.

It has been six years since we left Wickham, Jonathan thought. Six years since Abby died. And Papa is more obsessed with the Goodes than ever.

Jonathan ran his index finger along the freshly painted wall of their new house. The third house in six years, Jonathan thought bitterly.

Papa promised this would be the last move. We shall see. Every time we move he says he is positive he has found the Goodes—but still we have not found them yet.

Jonathan started down the stairs, his black shoes loud on the wooden steps. He wore white stockings with the buckled shoes and dark green knee breeches. His shirt was white cotton with a plain ruffle.

His mother no longer made his clothes—she had no need to. All the Fiers had their clothes made by a seamstress now.

The Fiers had grown rich in the last six years. Whenever they moved to a new town, Ezra brought with him some goods—tea, spices, fancy silks—to sell to the townspeople. His instinct for selling was uncanny. In each town Ezra knew exactly what the people would need.

Thanks to his ability, the family was now quite

comfortable. But their new wealth had not brought Ezra peace.

As Jonathan reached the bottom of the stairs, he heard a knock at the front door.

"I will answer it, Mama," he called. He could hear her in the kitchen, unpacking.

Jonathan opened the front door. There stood a very pretty girl who appeared to be about sixteen or seventeen years old.

She had smooth brown hair pulled back into a knot at the nape of her neck. She wore a simple green dress with white ruffles at the neckline and the sleeves. She gazed at Jonathan with lively brown eyes, and smiled.

"Good evening," said the girl, dropping into a quick curtsy. She held a round dish covered with a cloth in one hand. "My name is Delilah Wilson. I live on the farm down the road."

"Please come in," offered Jonathan.

"I know you moved in today, and I thought you might like something more with your supper," Delilah said. She held out the round dish as she stepped through the doorway. "I have brought you an apple pie."

Jonathan took the pie and thanked her. It was still warm.

"Please come into the parlor, Miss Wilson," he said. "I will tell my mother and father that you are here. I know they would like to meet you."

He showed Delilah into the parlor and took the pie into the kitchen to his mother.

"How kind of her," Jane Fier said. "Go get your father. We can have some pie and invite our new neighbor to share it with us."

Wiping her hands on her apron, she hurried to the parlor to meet Delilah. Jonathan knocked on the door of his father's study.

"Come in," his father called gruffly.

Jonathan opened the study door. Most of his father's books and maps, his business records, and the family Bible were still packed up in crates. Ezra sat at his desk facing the doorway bent over a map.

"What is it?" Ezra demanded impatiently. His black hair was shot through with pewter gray now, and the lines in his face had deepened.

He did not look up from his map of western Massachusetts. Jonathan knew his father was following a new trail that he imagined the Goodes might have taken.

"Papa, a young woman has come to see us. One of our neighbors."

"So?"

Jonathan cleared his throat. "Well, she would like to meet you."

"Not just now. I am busy."

Jonathan stood in the doorway for a moment, unsure of what to do next. The silver pendant his father always wore flashed in the candlelight, the blue stones gleaming. Ezra said, "Close the door behind you."

Jonathan started into the hall on his way back to the parlor. On his way he heard a light step on the stairs. He glanced up.

Rachel, dressed in a light summer nightgown, was creeping down the steps.

"Rachel!" cried Jonathan. "You heard Papa—"

Rachel raised a finger to her lips to quiet him. "Who

is here?" she whispered. "One of our neighbors? I want to meet her!"

"Papa will be very angry—"

But Rachel ignored him. She ran quickly down the stairs and slipped into the parlor, Jonathan right behind her.

His mother was talking to Delilah. When she saw Rachel, Jane Fier opened her eyes wide in astonishment and cried out—

"Abigail!"

Chapter
8

"What are you doing out of bed, Abby?" Jane Fier cried.

Jonathan watched as Rachel's young face grew solemn. He stepped forward and, putting a hand on Jane's shoulder, gently corrected his mother.

"It is Rachel, Mama. She wants to meet our new neighbor."

A shadow of confusion passed briefly across Jane Fier's face. Then it cleared.

She took Rachel's hand, patted it, and smiled.

Rachel relaxed and sat down.

I suppose poor Rachel is used to it by now, Jonathan thought sadly. Used to Mama's confusion.

Rachel did resemble Abigail, even though she was blond and Abby had had red hair.

Still, it is not their looks that confuses Mama, Jonathan realized. Abigail lives on in Mama's mind. Mama cannot let Abby die.

Delilah nodded toward the little girl and said, "I am happy to meet you, Rachel."

"My father is busy at the moment, I'm afraid," Jonathan told Delilah. "But he is very eager to meet you and your family. Perhaps he will call on you tomorrow."

Delilah nodded.

"Please excuse me for a moment," said Jane. "I will leave my son and daughter to entertain you while I prepare the pie, Miss Wilson."

Jonathan smiled. Somehow Rachel had gotten her way and would stay up to have pie with them.

Delilah, Jonathan, and Rachel took seats. The parlor was not fully furnished yet, just a couch and a few chairs clustered around a small table.

But Ezra had already hung a large painting over the fireplace—a portrait of Abigail. Ezra had painted it himself, from memory.

In the portrait Abigail was dressed as Ezra had last seen her, in a blue dress, wearing her white cap with the blue ribbons.

"You have a lovely house," Delilah said, glancing around admiringly. The house, large and elegant, was three stories, painted white with black shutters and surrounded by a white fence. It was the nicest house the Fiers had ever lived in.

"Where have you moved from?" Delilah asked.

"From Worcester," answered Jonathan. "And before that, Danbury."

"My goodness!" Delilah exclaimed. "Why have you moved so much?"

Jonathan hesitated. He certainly did not want to explain his father's obsession with the Goode family to this pretty neighbor. How could she ever understand?

But before he could stop her, Rachel blurted out in a low voice, "It is Papa. He says our family is cursed!"

"Rachel!" Jonathan cut in.

Delilah's eyes widened. "Cursed? What do you mean?"

"This is just a little girl's exaggeration," Jonathan interrupted, hoping to end the discussion then.

"No, it is not!" Rachel insisted. "Papa tells me about it every night before bed."

She pointed to the portrait of Abigail and said, "That girl was my sister. She died when I was little. One of the Goodes got her."

"Rachel—" Jonathan warned. But Delilah acted very interested and pressed Rachel to go on.

To Jonathan's dismay, Rachel told Delilah all about the family curse and the feud between the Goodes and the Fiers. Jonathan watched Delilah's face as she heard the horrible details. She turned pale as flour, and her eyes grew wide.

She will never want to see us again, he thought, and was surprised at his disappointment. He already liked this lively girl very much.

At last Jonathan said, "It is all nonsense, Miss Wilson. My father has been filling Rachel's head with these stories, and she takes them too seriously."

"So you do not believe in the curse?" Delilah asked him, locking her eyes onto his.

"There is no curse," Jonathan replied, frowning. "And there would be no feud if Papa would only let it die. This is all of his own making—he brings trouble on himself. Our constant quest for the Goodes has almost ruled our lives, but the Goodes themselves have done nothing to hurt us."

"What about Abigail?" Rachel demanded.

Jonathan paused. He didn't like to think about Abigail.

Abigail would still be alive if it were not for Papa's crazy ideas, he thought bitterly. Papa forced us to live in Wickham when no decent family should have stayed there.

Abigail's death was Papa's fault.

Jonathan tried to shake away his unpleasant thoughts. He turned his gaze on Delilah. She was studying the portrait of Abigail.

"Abigail looks a lot like you, Rachel," Delilah said.

"Most people say that," said Rachel, smiling at Jonathan.

"Perhaps we should talk about something else," Jonathan said uncomfortably.

"Do you have any brothers and sisters, Miss Wilson?" Rachel asked eagerly.

"Rachel, you may call me Delilah," Delilah said. She turned to Jonathan and added, "You may, too."

Jonathan thought he saw her blush slightly.

"I am an only child," she told Rachel. "My mother died when I was born. I live with my father. He is a minister, but his congregation is very small. We live on a small farm."

Jonathan studied her dress, made of homespun linen dyed pale green. For the first time he noticed how worn it was. The lace at the sleeves was frayed, and here and there the skirt was expertly patched.

She probably wore her best dress to come calling on us, Jonathan thought. She must be very poor. It does not matter. She is still the prettiest girl I have ever seen.

Jonathan walked into town a few days later to see the blacksmith. His mother wanted a new pot to hang over the kitchen fire.

He ordered the pot from the blacksmith and left the shop. Just outside he bumped into a pretty, brown-haired girl in a dark blue dress and white sunbonnet.

"Delilah Wilson! How pleasant to see you again."

"I am glad to see you, too, Jonathan." She carried a small basket. Jonathan took the basket to carry for her. It was empty.

"Where are you going?" he asked.

"I am on my way home," she replied. "I have just come from Papa's church. He has been there all morning with nothing to eat, so I brought him a bit of cheese and bread."

"I am on my way home, too, as it happens," said Jonathan. "May I escort you?"

Delilah smiled. "Thank you. That is very kind."

The afternoon sun shone bright and hot as they walked out of town and down the road to Delilah's house. Jonathan could feel himself begin to sweat under his collar.

"How is your family?" Delilah asked. "Your mother and sister?"

"Quite well, thank you," said Jonathan.

"I liked them both very much," Delilah went on. "Your sister especially. She is very sweet."

Jonathan felt a little uncomfortable at the memory of Delilah's visit—his mother's confusion, Rachel's talk of a family curse. Delilah is being polite, he decided. She must think us very strange.

"I must apologize for Rachel's behavior the other evening," he said. "I hope she did not frighten you—or bore you—with her silly talk."

Delilah laughed. "Not at all. She is only a child, and children love wild stories. I was exactly the same at her age."

"I am sure you were much more sensible than Rachel," Jonathan protested.

"If anything I was sillier. Just ask my father. At eight I was sure that a fox would come in my window in the night to carry me off. I insisted that we keep all the windows in the house shut at night—even when it was quite hot. My father thought I had gone mad!"

Jonathan smiled at her story and offered her his arm. She accepted, and together they walked arm in arm.

That night Jonathan lay in bed a long time without sleeping. An image of Delilah floated before his eyes: her glossy brown hair, her creamy skin, her rosy cheeks, her mischievous brown eyes.

I shall call on her tomorrow, he thought, growing sleepy at last. I will bring a bouquet of flowers. . . .

A sudden noise made him sit straight up.

What was that?

The sound seemed to be far off. Had he been dreaming?

No. There it was again. Closer now.

Jonathan listened. The sound started low but quickly grew in pitch and volume. At first he thought it was some kind of animal shriek, a tortured cry, a scream of agony.

Jonathan shook with fear. He had never heard any animal make that sound.

Was it a bear? A wolf? An injured dog?

It was moving swiftly toward his house, nearer, nearer.

Now it was right in the yard, and coming closer.

It stopped right under his window!

Jonathan's heart leapt to his throat.

A voice in his head screamed, "Help! Please, somebody—help! It is coming to get me!"

Chapter
9

His heart thudding in his chest, Jonathan stumbled to the window. The full moon shone on the wide rose trellis—still barren of roses—that climbed the back wall of the house to the second-floor windows.

He could see the backyard clearly—the woodpile, the new iron pump, the stone well, and the woods surrounding them.

What made that horrible sound? Jonathan asked himself, trembling all over. Was it only a dream? A strange wild animal? Or was it something more terrible still?

He pushed that idea from his mind. Rachel's stories are giving *me* nightmares, he scolded himself.

Silence now. The only sounds were the chirping of crickets and the low hooting of an owl. Still shaken, Jonathan climbed back into bed.

He knew he would *never* get to sleep now. He lay awake all night, listening.

Hours later the sky began to lighten. Jonathan heard his mother pass his room on her way downstairs to begin the day's chores. His father and sister were stirring, too.

Yawning and stretching, Jonathan climbed out of bed and sleepily made his way to the washstand. He splashed cold water on his face and ran a comb through his shoulder-length brown hair. After tying his hair back with a black cord, he slipped on his knee breeches.

In the kitchen Jane Fier was setting dishes on the table. "Good morning, Jonathan," she said brightly. "Would you mind kindling the fire for me?"

Jonathan kissed his mother good morning and went to the hearth. He picked up the bellows and puffed air into the glowing embers left over from the night before.

Rachel skipped into the room in a brown dress and apron, her blond curls bouncing. Ezra followed close behind her. As he poked at the fire, Jonathan wondered whether any of them had heard the terrible cries that had awakened him in the night. Rachel appeared to be cheerful and well rested, but Ezra seemed tired.

"Run out to the well and get me a bucket of water, Rachel," said Jane.

"Yes, Mama," Rachel replied. She opened the back door and headed out to the well.

A moment later bloodcurdling cries from the backyard made Jonathan drop his fireplace poker. It clattered to the hearth floor as he turned to run outside. Jane and Ezra were right behind him.

Rachel stood by the well, screaming hysterically.

Her hands, her face, her hair, her clothes were all splattered in red.

"Abigail—what *is* it?" cried Jane. "What has happened?"

Rachel ignored her mother. Her eyes fixed and staring, she pointed at the bucket she had pulled out of the well.

Peering into the bucket, Jonathan gagged.

It was filled with thick, red blood.

Chapter
10

Holding his hand over his mouth, Jonathan reeled backward.

Blood! How could the well be full of blood?

Trying not to vomit, Jonathan raised his eyes to his family. Jane was holding Rachel, trying to comfort her. Ezra's eyes were bulging and his hand shook as he clutched his silver pendant.

"The curse!" he cried. "The Goodes have come for us again!"

Swallowing hard, Jonathan gathered his courage and reluctantly peered into the well. To his relief, the well water was clean.

Only the bucket was filled with blood.

What did it mean?

Her arms around her shoulders, Jane gently guided Rachel inside. Ezra nervously rubbed his fingers over the pendant, as if it would help him somehow.

"It has happened again. They have found us before

we could find them," Ezra said. "There must be Goodes living nearby—or buried near here."

"Calm down, Papa," Jonathan pleaded. "There is no curse. Look—we are all safe."

"Foolish boy," Ezra murmured, and he left his son alone.

Still dazed and shaken, Jonathan stared at the bucket of blood. The howl of agony he had heard in the night came rushing back to him.

Who, or what, could have done this? he wondered.

Was it the work of a crazy person? A wild animal?

Or could his father be right after all? Could it really be the curse of the Goodes?

Rachel stayed in her room for the rest of the morning while Ezra paced the house, tense and scowling.

I must get out of here, Jonathan told himself. As long as I sit in this house, I shall keep seeing that bucket of blood.

He decided to pay a call on Delilah.

Jonathan gathered wildflowers as he walked down the road to the little farmhouse. It was very small—only a cabin really—and shabby, made of brown-weathered shingles, with only a few small windows and one chimney.

To the right of the house sat a tumbledown cow shed. A few chickens pecked at the dirt behind a fence. Beyond them were a stand of scraggly fruit trees and an acre or two of stony fields.

Clutching his handful of purple and white flowers, Jonathan knocked on the door. Delilah opened it.

"Hello, Jonathan," she said, smiling. "What a nice surprise."

As he handed her the flowers, he felt his face grow hot.

She invited him in. A man with shoulder-length gray hair sat at a writing table in a corner of the room. He stood up when Jonathan entered.

"Father, this is Jonathan Fier," Delilah said. "Jonathan, this is my father, the Reverend Wilson."

Delilah's father gave Jonathan a friendly handshake. "I am very pleased to meet you, young man," the reverend said. "I plan to call on your parents soon to welcome them."

"They will be delighted," Jonathan said with a polite bow.

"Father is working on a sermon at the moment," Delilah said. "Shall we go for a walk?"

Jonathan agreed. He and Delilah went outside and strolled through the orchard of fruit trees.

In the warm sunlight Jonathan thought Delilah was prettier than ever. Her cheeks glowed pink, and she had a lively spring to her step.

But as she looked at his face, he saw her frown. "You look tired, Jonathan," she said. "Are you feeling well?"

Jonathan started to say, "Yes, of course." But then he thought better of it. Delilah has already heard all about the family history, he thought, and she is not afraid of me. Not in the least afraid. She is an understanding girl. Perhaps I have found someone I can speak with—at last!

"Something disturbed me last night, while I was sleeping," he told her. "A strange and terrifying noise."

"A noise?" she asked, puzzled.

"Yes. It was as if some hideous creature were

ushing through the woods, heading straight for our house. It drew closer until it seemed to be right under my window, shrieking. Then suddenly it stopped."

"What was it?" Delilah asked.

"I do not know," Jonathan replied. "When I looked outside, I saw nothing."

"It must have been a dream," Delilah told him.

"That is what I decided," Jonathan said. "But this morning Rachel went to the well for water, and when she pulled up the bucket—" He paused, wondering if he should continue. Should he say such a shocking thing to a young lady he hardly knew?

Delilah stopped walking and faced him. "What happened?" she asked. "What did you find in the bucket?"

"It was full of blood," he told her.

Delilah gasped.

"My father is convinced that it has something to do with the curse," Jonathan said. "I cannot help but wonder if he is right."

Now Delilah turned her face away. "Oh, no," she said, walking ahead of him. Were her hands shaking? Jonathan could not be sure. "He cannot be right about this, can he, Jonathan? There must be some reasonable explanation."

"There must be," Jonathan said. "But I cannot think of one. Do you suppose a wounded animal somehow got into the well? But that does not make sense. There was so much blood—and no sign of an animal. And the well water was perfectly clean."

Delilah stopped again and took Jonathan's hand. "Please, Jonathan," she pleaded. "Forget about this curse. Let it be your father's obsession, not yours."

Jonathan put his hand over hers. Her skin was so

soft. Her words echoed in his mind. Forget about thi curse, he thought. That is exactly what I would hav said—until today.

He and Delilah walked on in silence.

She is a very sensible girl, Jonathan thought. I an glad we have met. It is so good to have someone t confide in.

That night Jonathan went to bed early and immedi ately fell asleep.

Deep in the night a noise woke him.

Creak.

Jonathan's eyes flew open. He listened, holding hi breath.

It was the dead of night. The house lay bathed i darkness.

Creak.

Jonathan's heart began to pound. There it wa again.

Creak. Creak.

It came from the hall. His mouth suddenly dry, hi temples throbbing, Jonathan slipped out of bed and crept to the door.

He put his ear to the door and listened. I really di hear a noise this time, he thought. I am sure of it.

Creeeeak.

Slowly, silently, he opened the door. The hall wa dark. He listened to footsteps quietly coming towar him.

He peered around the door and into the hall.

There it stood.

His blood stopped flowing in his veins.

At the end of the hall he saw a vision in white— floating toward him.

Chapter
11

"Who is it?" Jonathan cried. But his voice came out a choked whisper.

The pale figure whispered, "Abigail! Abigail!"

It floated closer. Jonathan could see a white nightgown and white nightcap, long gray hair flowing under it. He heard the floorboards creaking under her bare feet.

It cannot be a ghost, he thought.

The apparition called out softly, "Abigail! Abigail! Come back!"

It is Mama, Jonathan realized, alarmed. What is she doing?

His mother stepped quietly past him, not seeing him. Again she called, "Abigail!"

She is walking in her sleep, Jonathan realized.

She started down the stairs and Jonathan followed.

She made her way to the back of the house, the

ghostly white gown trailing along the floor. "Abigail!" she called a little louder this time. "Wait for me!"

She opened the back door. She was going outside.

Jonathan stepped forward and grabbed her arm. "Mama!" he cried in a trembling voice. "What are you doing?"

She turned around, startled. Her eyes were wide open and full of tears.

She is not asleep, Jonathan thought. She is awake. She knows what she is doing.

"It is Abigail," his mother whispered, tears rolling down her quivering cheeks. "She called to me. She is out there, waiting for me."

Jonathan pulled his mother inside and closed the door. "No, Mama," he said, desperate to soothe her. "You must be dreaming."

"I am not dreaming, Jonathan." His mother's voice was firm now. "She is in the backyard. My little girl . . ."

Jonathan opened the door and peered outside. It was a warm, clear night, well lit by the moon. He saw no one outside. No sign of Abigail.

"No one is there, Mama," Jonathan said. "Please, you must go back to bed."

He put an arm around his mother's shoulders and began to lead her back to the stairs. She struggled against him.

"No!" she cried. "Abigail needs me!"

Jonathan was stronger and guided his mother upstairs. "You cannot go outside—you will catch cold. You had a bad dream, Mama. That is all," he said. "Just a bad dream."

But no matter what he told her, Jane refused to believe that her dead daughter hadn't called to her.

She allowed herself to be taken upstairs, but still she was frantic with grief and worry. She went to bed, and at last, exhausted, fell into a deep sleep.

Jonathan shut the door to his room and went to his window to look out. The yard, with the woods behind it, stretched quiet and peaceful in the moonlight.

In the morning the Fier family went about their chores as if it were any other day. Neither Jonathan nor his mother said a word to anyone about what had happened the night before.

It was almost as if it really *had* been a dream. Jonathan knew better.

Mama has been shaken since Abigail died, Jonathan thought. But it has always been a matter of a momentary confusion. She has never gone this far before.

The next night he lay awake, waiting for a noise. Hours passed in peaceful stillness. Jonathan's body began to relax. Then, just as he began to feel drowsy, he heard it.

Creak.

"Abigail! Abigail!" came the whispered cry.

He heard his father's heavier tread on the floorboards.

"Jane, come back to bed," Ezra whispered. "You will wake up the children."

Jonathan heard his father take his mother back into their room and shut the door. He heard their muffled voices, then his mother crying.

Jonathan's mother stayed in bed all the next day, and the next. But at night she roamed the house, calling for her dead daughter.

"I want to do something for her," Rachel told Jonathan. "Something to cheer her up."

Jonathan sighed. He doubted anything he or Rachel could do would make their mother happy.

"What about the trellis?" Rachel suggested. "We could plant roses. Someday they will grow so high they will reach her bedroom window."

"All right," Jonathan agreed. He was glad to get out of the house, at least.

Jonathan took a shovel and Rachel took a spade. They began to dig holes for the rosebushes.

Feeling a light tap on his shoulder, Jonathan whirled around to see who was there.

He found himself staring into Delilah's pretty face.

"Good afternoon," she said.

"Good afternoon," Jonathan answered.

"Hello, Delilah!" Rachel called.

Jonathan wiped his dirty hands on his work pants and wished Delilah had not found him so muddy. But she did not seem to mind.

"Do you two have time for a visitor?" Delilah asked.

"Of course," said Jonathan.

"I need a rest anyway," Rachel said. "I am tired of digging."

"Shall we sit in the shade?" Jonathan suggested.

Jonathan and Delilah sat under an apple tree while Rachel ran off and was soon back with a pitcher of lemon water.

"I have come to see how the two of you are doing," said Delilah. "I have been worried about you."

Jonathan was silent. But Rachel said, "Oh, Delilah —Mama is not well. She walks through the house every night, calling for Abigail. We think she sees Abigail's ghost!"

Delilah's eyes widened, and she raised a hand to her throat. She turned to Jonathan. "Can this be true?"

"It is true that Mama is upset," Jonathan told her. "Every night she cries out for Abigail. She—she says she sees Abigail in the yard, beckoning to her."

Delilah sucked in her breath and shut her eyes. "This is dreadful," she murmured, almost as if she were talking to herself.

Jonathan leaned closer to her. "But I am sure it is not a ghost," he said to reassure her. "Please do not worry about us, Delilah. Rachel exaggerates sometimes."

"I do not!" cried Rachel.

A bit of color returned to Delilah's face, and she grew calmer.

"She could be dreaming, could she not?" she suggested. "The same dream, night after night?"

Jonathan sipped his lemon water thoughtfully. He studied Delilah's face, and she smiled at him.

She is so brave, he thought. She is trying to make Rachel and me feel better.

Rachel is afraid of a ghost, and I am afraid that my mother is going insane. Delilah does not want us to be frightened, so she assures us it is a dream.

"Jonathan."

Jonathan's eyes flew open. It was the middle of the night.

Another sound.

Mama?

"Jonathan," came the eerie whisper. "Jonathan—beware!"

Jonathan froze as he stared into the darkness.

It was not his mother, but the soft, sweet voice of a girl.

"Who is there?" he whispered.

"Beware, my brother," came the girl's voice. It seemed to be coming from outside the open window. But that was impossible. . . .

"Beware, my brother," the voice said again. "Or your fate will be worse than mine!"

Jonathan sat up. "Rachel?" he called. "Rachel? Where are you?"

"No," whispered the little girl. "No, not Rachel. I am Abigail."

Chapter
12

Jonathan jumped out of bed. "Abigail!" he cried frantically. "Abigail! Where are you?"

He froze in the center of the room and listened.

No one answered. The voice was gone.

His hands trembling, Jonathan lit a candle from the smoldering embers in the fireplace. The candlelight made his shadow rise eerily on the wall.

Jonathan searched every corner of the room. He threw open the wardrobe door and peered inside.

No sign of his dead sister. No sign of anyone.

His heart thumping, Jonathan slumped back onto the bed.

Abigail had called to him. Or *had* she?

Had it been another dream?

Perhaps Mama's madness is getting to me, he thought. But he quickly dismissed the idea.

The voice was real. I did hear Abigail calling me, warning me about something. . . .

Then a soft tapping at his door startled him.

He leapt to his feet, staring at the door.

Should he open it?

He had no time to decide. The door squeaked open slowly.

In walked Rachel.

She wore her nightshift and cap, her feet bare. Her eyes in the dim candlelight were round with fear.

"Rachel, what is it?" Jonathan asked, his voice a low whisper.

"I saw her!" Rachel cried. "I saw Abigail!"

Chapter
13

Jonathan rushed to his sister and took her by the shoulders. "You saw Abigail?" he said. "Where?"

"I saw her face outside my window. She called to me, 'Rachel! Beware!'"

"But how did you know it was Abigail?" Jonathan asked. "Do you remember what she looked like?"

"She looked like Papa's picture of her," said Rachel. "She wore a white cap with blue ribbons, and she was floating outside my window. Then she disappeared."

Jonathan let go of Rachel. Maybe Mama really had seen Abigail, he thought. Perhaps she saw what Rachel saw. It *had* to be Abigail. Abigail's ghost.

Abigail had come to warn her family.

But of what?

* * *

"I am going to call on the Wilsons, Mama," Jonathan told Jane. She sat by the hearth in the kitchen, too tired to move.

"Let me go with you," Rachel begged. "I like Delilah."

"Not today, Rachel," said Jonathan. "Today I want to see her alone."

Their mother gave Jonathan a basket of sweet rolls to take with him as a gift. "Please send our regards to her father," Jane said. Then she sighed. "We should have had them to tea by now, but it has been so difficult. . . ."

Tears welled up in her eyes, which she brushed away. Misery had aged Jonathan's mother since Abigail's death. The corners of her mouth sagged, and her eyes were dull and almost colorless. Jonathan noticed that the past few days had sharpened the pain in her face.

"Apologize to the Wilsons for me," she went on. "And tell them—tell them I have been ill."

"I will," Jonathan promised. He put a hand on her arm and added, "You will feel better soon, Mama. I know you will."

She nodded absently. Jonathan took the basket and set off down the road to the Wilsons' farm.

The Reverend Wilson was working in a field when Jonathan arrived, but Delilah's lively face lifted Jonathan's spirits. She took the rolls with a smile. "It was so thoughtful of your mother to send them," she said. "How is she?"

Jonathan sighed. "No better," he told her. "She still sees Abigail at night. But now, at least, she is not the only one."

"What do you mean?"

"Rachel saw her, too. And I—well, I heard Abigail's voice. She called to me."

Delilah dropped the basket and turned her face away. Jonathan saw her shoulders shaking under her faded pink dress.

"Delilah, what is wrong?" Gently he turned her around, put his arms on her shoulders to stop their shaking, and gazed intently into her eyes. But she lowered her face as if she didn't want him to see her expression.

When she finally raised her eyes, they were filled with tears. "I am very worried about you, Jonathan," she said. "About you and your family. I—I would never wish any harm on you, ever."

Jonathan thought she was even prettier than usual with her eyes shining with tears. He wanted to throw his arms around her and kiss her.

"What are you talking about, Delilah?" he asked. "I know you wouldn't wish harm on us. This has nothing to do with you." He paused, feeling guilty. "I should never have burdened you with our problems, Delilah. You are taking them upon yourself."

Delilah closed her eyes. "My father and I are leaving soon," she said quietly. "Perhaps, once we are gone—"

"No!" Jonathan cried. "You cannot leave! Please!"

He was surprised to hear himself speak these words. The idea of Delilah's leaving was painful. He felt as if he had been punched in the stomach.

I am in love with her, he realized right then. *Completely, desperately in love with her.*

He took her hands in his and demanded, "Why? Why must you leave? Please, Delilah, stay here. . . ."

She lowered her head again. "It is for the best,

Jonathan. You must believe me. By the end of the week we will be gone."

"Delilah, I do not understand—"

"Please go now, Jonathan," she said with a tremor in her voice. "Please—you must leave."

Jonathan made his way from the Wilsons' cottage and trudged home with a heavy heart. I love her, he thought miserably. And I know she loves me, too. I know it. So why must she leave? Why can't she explain? Why is she so sad, and so mysterious?

That night Jonathan waited to hear his mother's whispered cries. He tried to force his eyes open, to remain alert.

But after so many sleepless nights, he couldn't stay awake. He drifted off into a heavy and dreamless sleep.

Then, just before dawn, a horrifying scream pierced his sleep-fogged brain.

Jonathan jerked straight up in bed. The scream had come from the backyard.

He hurried to the window. The first pink light of morning was beginning to show on the horizon. Squinting into the yard, he could see nothing unusual.

The scream lingered in his mind, echoed in his ears. None of the horrors of the past few weeks had prepared him for the terrible agony in that scream.

Jonathan heard footsteps on the stairs. He crept to the door. In the gray light he saw Ezra and Rachel heading downstairs. Jonathan followed.

Where is Mama? he thought. Panic rose in his throat. He pushed it down, swallowed it. No time for panic.

Jonathan followed his father and sister outside. The

yard was silent now. But they had all heard the scream. They all agreed it had come from the yard.

"Where is Mama?" Jonathan asked his father.

"I do not know," Ezra said. "That scream woke me up, and she was not there. I cannot help but think—" Ezra glanced at Rachel. He did not finish his sentence.

"Do not worry, Papa," Jonathan said. "We will find her."

For hours they searched the house, every inch of it. Jane was not there. The sun was rising above the trees now.

They dressed quickly and returned to the yard, searching around every bush, behind every tree.

Rachel stood at the edge of the woods, calling for her mother. Jonathan felt tired and discouraged.

What could have happened to my mother? he wondered. How could she vanish into thin air?

His mouth felt dry as cotton. He made his way to the well for a drink. As he tugged on the rope to pull up the bucket, the rope felt strangely heavy.

A wave of dread swept over Jonathan.

"Papa!" he called hoarsely. "Come help me pull up the well bucket."

Ezra narrowed his eyes at Jonathan but said nothing. He stepped beside his son. Together, their faces set in hard concentration, they heaved on the rope.

"It is so heavy, Papa," Jonathan said, pulling with all his strength. "I cannot imagine—"

One final tug.

Jonathan gasped in disbelief.

And then he started to scream.

Chapter
14

Jonathan's scream roared over the yard.

"What is it? What is it?" Rachel cried shrilly, running to the well.

Jonathan was too horrified to reply. Too horrified to move. Too horrified to pull his eyes away from the gruesome sight before him.

At the end of the well rope, sprawled over the bucket, was the body of his mother.

Her skin was blue and bloated. Her wet hair plastered against her skull and face. Her soaked nightgown clung tightly to her lifeless form.

"No! No! *No!*"

Jonathan's sobs wrenched his throat.

"Mama!" Rachel whispered. "Mama—why?"

Jonathan's father held on to the bucket with both hands. His eyes were shut. His lips moved in a silent prayer.

"No! No!"

Trying to turn his gaze away, Jonathan saw something. Something gripped tightly in his mother's closed fist.

He reached down and pried open the cold, bloated fingers.

"Ohhh!" Jonathan gasped when he saw it.

A white cap with blue ribbons.

"Mama! Mama!" Rachel repeated. She dropped to her knees in front of her mother and began to sob.

Without a word, Jonathan helped Ezra lift Jane's body and set it down on the grass.

Can that really be my mother? Jonathan asked through a blur of tears. Can that really be my mother so cold, so still?

He picked up his little sister and carried her, sobbing, into the house.

There is no doubt in my mind now, Jonathan thought later. The Fier family is cursed. I did not want to believe it. But Papa has been right all along.

The hair prickled on the back of his neck. In a flash Jonathan suddenly understood.

Delilah's strange sadness . . . Her sudden desire to leave, to get away from the Fiers . . . It all fell into place like the pieces of a puzzle.

Jonathan ran past where his father sat slumped at the table, his head buried in his hands, and out into the yard.

Rachel's face appeared in her bedroom window. "Where are you going?" she called down to him.

Jonathan did not answer her. Instead, he started to run. Glancing back, he saw Rachel following him, but he didn't stop to send her home.

Jonathan ran down the road to the Wilsons' farm. Delilah was in the yard, feeding the chickens.

As he came into view, she dropped the sack of feed. He grabbed her hands and held them tight.

"Delilah, my love!" he cried breathlessly. "You must tell me. You must tell me your secret."

She stared at him, startled.

Rachel arrived, panting, holding her side from running so hard.

Jonathan ignored her. He did not care who was there, who heard what he had asked. He had to know if he was right. He had to know *now*.

"I already know your secret," he told Delilah. "Just tell me yourself."

He gazed deeply into her brown eyes.

"Yes," she replied quietly. "I can see it in your face, Jonathan. You know my terrible secret, don't you?"

She shut her eyes, a tear falling onto her cheek.

"I am a Goode," she confessed.

Chapter
15

Jonathan stared at her. He opened his mouth to speak, but no sound came out.

"How can you be a Goode?" Rachel demanded. "I thought your name was Wilson."

"We—we changed our name," Delilah explained. "We once lived in another town, near Boston. But when word of the plague in Wickham reached our town, our neighbors drove us out. They had heard rumors that the Goodes were responsible for the plague, so they shunned us. We moved west—and Father changed our name. We became the Wilsons."

Jonathan suddenly felt dizzy. He rubbed his temples with his fingers.

"I wanted to tell you my name was Goode," Delilah said. "I knew I should be honest. But I liked you both so much. I did not want to scare you away. And I thought that maybe—maybe there really was no curse."

She paused and gazed at Jonathan.

"You did not believe in the curse," she said softly to him. "And you are so smart and kind. I thought that if you did not believe in it, then it could not be true."

"I did not want to believe it," Jonathan said. "I wanted to be happy."

A sad smile crossed Delilah's face. "I am afraid we cannot deny it any longer," she whispered. "There is a curse on your family. A curse on both our families." She swallowed hard. "There is only one way to stop it."

Jonathan's heart pounded harder. "There is a way to stop it?" he demanded breathlessly, hardly daring to hope it was true. "What is it?"

Delilah avoided his eyes. "It involves some sacrifice," she said, blushing. "On your part."

"I will do anything!" Jonathan cried. "Please, Delilah. Tell me how to break the curse."

She took a deep breath. "The feuding families must unite. They must form an unshakable bond."

"How?" Jonathan asked.

"Marriage," Delilah replied, still avoiding his eyes. "A Goode and a Fier must marry."

"But that is very simple," Rachel interrupted. "You two can get married."

Kneeling, Jonathan took Delilah's hand and kissed it joyfully. "How can you call that a sacrifice, Delilah? I am already in love with you. You must know that by now. I love you so much I would marry you even if it brought a *new* curse down on me and my family!"

Tears streamed down Delilah's cheeks. "Jonathan—"

He stopped her. "Please, dear Delilah, before you

say another word—I must ask for your hand in marriage."

She smiled through her tears and struggled to speak. "I love you, too, Jonathan," she replied softly. "But I am afraid—"

"What are you afraid of?" he asked. "You are not afraid of *me,* are you?"

"No, I am not afraid of you. I am afraid of the curse. I am afraid that something could happen—something terrible—to stop our wedding."

"Nothing can stop me from marrying you!" Jonathan declared, rising to his feet. "And to make sure of that, we shall marry as soon as possible. Your father can marry us. He is a minister. He can do it *today,* before anything can happen."

Delilah's face lit up. Smiling, she wiped the tears from her cheeks. "He is at the church right now. Oh, Jonathan, I am so happy! I can hardly believe this is happening."

Jonathan smiled at her, but deep inside him a question still burned. Could this marriage really end the curse—once and for all? Could that be possible?

"We will be sisters, Delilah!" Rachel exclaimed. "I will bear witness at the ceremony."

Jonathan had almost forgotten his sister was there. "No, Rachel," he ordered. "Run home and stay with Papa. He will be wondering where you are now—and he must not find you here. Run home—please. Hurry!"

In the tiny clapboard church Jonathan gripped Delilah's hand. Her father, the Reverend Wilson, stood behind a simple altar, facing them, a worn black leather Bible in his hands.

"I, Jonathan, take thee, Delilah . . ."

Jonathan repeated the minister's words, hardly knowing what he said. His heart was racing. His only desire was to get safely through the ceremony—and then to hold his new wife in his arms.

Now Delilah repeated the vows.

Jonathan stole a glance at his beautiful bride. He only wished his mother was still alive to share this moment.

The ceremony was nearly over. In moments I will be married, he thought.

And the curse will be ended. The Fiers and the Goodes will be joined.

The Reverend Wilson cleared his throat. "If anyone knows of just cause why these two should not be united in holy matrimony, let him speak now, or forever hold his peace."

Silence.

Then a startling crash.

Spinning around, Jonathan saw that the doors of the small church had flown open.

Silhouetted against the bright daylight outside, a man came into focus.

What is that in his hand? Jonathan wondered, squinting into the bright rectangle of light.

A rifle?

Ezra!

"Stop at once!" Ezra screamed. He burst into the church and strode up the aisle, rifle in hand.

Rachel burst in behind him. "Jonathan, I am sorry!" she cried, her voice shrill with fear. "Papa made me tell! I am sorry!"

The little girl tugged desperately at her father's arm, trying to hold him back. Ezra pushed his daughter roughly aside and continued down the aisle, his eyes narrowed on Jonathan, his features set in hard fury.

"Stop this wedding!" he demanded. He stopped and raised the rifle to his shoulder. "All Goodes must die!"

Jonathan felt his heart skip. "Papa—no!" he screamed.

With a desperate cry he dived toward his father and grabbed the gun, trying to take it from him.

They struggled.

Delilah raised her hands to her face and screamed.

"Traitor!" Ezra snarled bitterly to his son. "How could you do this to me?"

"Papa—give me the gun!" Jonathan demanded.

The two men wrestled over it, their shoes scuffling over the wooden floorboards.

"Give it to me!" Jonathan pleaded.

He tugged hard and pulled the rifle free.

As Jonathan staggered back with it, the rifle went off.

"Ohhh!" Jonathan uttered a startled cry as the sound echoed through the tiny church.

He heard a sharp cry.

And turned to the altar.

Delilah stood as if suspended by wires, her features twisted in shock and horror.

A red stain appeared on the front of her white dress.

Jonathan stared helplessly as the stain darkened and spread.

I've shot Delilah, he realized.

87

Chapter
16

"Delilah!"

Jonathan screamed her name in a choked voice he didn't recognize, and let the rifle fall.

Before he could run to her, Delilah's eyelids slid shut. She uttered a faint gasp and slumped to the floor.

Jonathan dropped beside her. "Delilah! Delilah!"

He called her name again and again.

But, he knew, she could not hear him now.

The dark blood puddled beneath her white dress.

"Oh, Delilah," Jonathan sobbed, cradling her head in his arms.

Behind him, Jonathan heard a click. He turned.

Ezra had picked up the rifle, which he was now pointing at the minister's head.

"All Goodes will die," Ezra said calmly, hate burning in his eyes.

The Reverend Wilson fell to his knees beside his

daughter's lifeless body. "Please do not shoot me!" he cried. "Please!"

Jonathan gently laid Delilah's body on the floor and stepped toward his father. "Papa, please—"

Ezra leveled the rifle at Jonathan. "Do not get in my way again, son," he growled, his voice hard and sharp as a steel blade. "I am warning you."

Jonathan said nothing. Ezra turned back to the minister. "All Goodes will die," he repeated.

Reverend Wilson clasped his hands together as if in prayer. "Please do not shoot me," he begged again. "I am not a Goode!"

"Your lies will not succeed with me," Ezra snapped. "You cannot save yourself. My wife is dead because of you—and now you must pay the price."

Delilah's father shook in terror. "It is true! I swear to you! I am not a Goode. Delilah was not a Goode either!"

He turned to Jonathan and added, "Jonathan—she lied to you!"

Chapter
17

"What are you *saying?*" Jonathan cried in disbelief.

"Do not listen to him, boy," Ezra urged coldly. "He is only looking for a way to save himself."

"I am telling the truth!" the minister insisted. "It was all a trick. A fraud! I *swear* it!"

Jonathan ignored his father and the rifle. "A trick?" he repeated weakly, grabbing the front of Reverend Wilson's robe. "A trick?"

"I—I wanted Delilah to marry you, Jonathan," the minister sputtered, his eyes on Ezra's rifle. "We are so poor, you see. And you are so well off. Delilah—she came home and told me the story of your feud with the Goodes. I—I had an idea. I saw a way we could use it—to trick you into marrying her."

"To trick me . . ." Jonathan murmured.

"I made her do it!" the minister cried. "I forced her

to." He lowered his gaze to his daughter's body. He stared at it for a moment as if he just realized she was dead. Then, with a shudder, he pulled his eyes away.

"Delilah was a good girl at heart," Reverend Wilson muttered. "A good girl."

"This is all nonsense!" Ezra snarled. "Prepare to die, Goode! I have waited so long, so long—all my life—for this chance. You will not cheat me of my revenge with your desperate lies."

"Please, Papa," Jonathan begged, pushing the rifle aside. "Let him speak."

"I forced Delilah to pretend that she was a Goode," Reverend Wilson confessed sadly. "But I knew you would not marry her just because of that. So she made you think your dead sister was haunting you. She made terrible screaming noises at night. Delilah filled your well bucket with chicken blood. She made a cap with blue ribbons on it, like the one she saw in a painting of your sister. And she climbed your rose trellis to appear in your windows at night."

Ezra lowered the rifle. His face grew red and his jaw trembled as he listened.

"Delilah lured your mother outside with that blue-ribboned cap," the minister continued in a quivering voice. "She threw it into the well. Your mother leaned over to retrieve it. And—she fell into the well. . . ."

He swallowed hard. "Delilah tried to help her, but she couldn't reach her."

He stopped again. He was breathing noisily, his chest heaving under his dark robe.

"Why?" Jonathan asked. "Why did you make Delilah do all this?"

"We had to frighten you, to make you desperate,"

answered the clergyman. "So desperate you would do anything to stop the horrors. So desperate you would marry Delilah. We were so poor, you see. So poor—"

"But I loved her," said Jonathan. "I would have married her anyway."

He dropped to his knees beside Delilah's dead body. Her mouth had fallen open, and a trickle of blood ran down her chin. Jonathan stared at the body as if it belonged to a stranger.

The minister shuddered violently now. "I know you cannot forgive me," he pleaded with Ezra, "but please, please do not kill me!"

Ezra's face hung slack. The anger faded from his eyes. The rifle fell from his hands and clattered on the church floor.

"My wife—my daughter—" he murmured. "The curse . . ."

His face had become as pale as Delilah's. His thin lips barely moved as he whispered, "The curse. The Fiers are truly cursed. . . ."

His hands flew to his head and he uttered a sorrowful wail and tore at his graying hair. Then he ran from the church, screaming.

Jonathan heard a horse whinny. Then a piercing scream, and finally a sickening crunch.

Chapter
18

"What was that?" Jonathan cried, knowing the answer to his question.

He ran outside. A small crowd had gathered around a horse and wagon.

Jonathan shouted, "Papa! Papa!" and pushed through the silent crowd.

"Papa!" Jonathan cried, seeing Ezra sprawled on his back, a dark open wound in his side, blood puddling on the dirt street.

"Get the doctor!" someone cried. "This man has been trampled!"

Jonathan knelt beside his father. Ezra's eyes rolled around blindly for a second. Then they focused on Jonathan.

Ezra lifted his hand and let it fall on the silver amulet.

"Take this," he whispered to Jonathan. He closed his eyes for a moment, gathering his strength. "Jonathan—" His voice grew weak. "The power of the Fiers is in this amulet. You must wear it always. Use it—use it to avenge my death."

Ezra took one last, shuddering breath. Then blood poured from his mouth. His eyes froze in a fixed and lifeless stare.

"Papa—" cried Jonathan. "Papa . . ."

Jonathan buried his face in his hands and sank deeply into his sorrow.

So many people have died, he thought. Abigail, Mama, Delilah, Papa. All because of this dreaded curse.

His father's strange silver pendant glinted in the sun.

The curse dies with my father, Jonathan thought. I will put an end to it, here and now.

No minister would give Ezra a funeral or allow his body to be buried in a church cemetery. He had been insane, a murderer, Reverend Wilson had warned. So Jonathan had Ezra's body cremated. Now all that remained of Ezra was a jar of ashes.

Rachel cried herself to sleep. Jonathan listened helplessly to her sobs, every cry torturing him.

He sat by the hearth, waiting for her crying to stop. At last the house grew still, and he knew she was asleep.

He took Ezra's ashes and poured them into an iron strongbox. Then he picked up the silver pendant.

To Jonathan's surprise, the pendant grew hot in his hand. He saw flames, flames he thought would swallow him up.

But the flames died as quickly as they had appeared. And the jeweled pendant cooled.

Jonathan examined the pendant, felt its weight against his palm.

His father's last words echoed in his mind. "Use it—to avenge my death."

No, thought Jonathan. No more revenge. No more feud. No more curse.

"I am sorry, Papa," he whispered. "But I cannot let our family suffer any longer. There is still Rachel. . . ."

He thought of his little sister, sleeping upstairs in her bedroom. She had already been through so much. But she might have a chance at happiness still. At least, Jonathan hoped so. He would do everything in his power to make her happy.

The first step, he decided, was to get rid of the pendant.

He dropped it into the strongbox. It landed softly on top of Ezra's ashes. Jonathan closed the heavy iron lid and locked it.

Then he took a lantern from its hook by the hearth. He made his way out into the night. He knelt beneath the apple tree. With a spade, he began to dig up the moist earth.

Bitter memories leapt to his mind as he worked under the tree. He tried to force them away as soon as they arose, but they kept coming back.

He remembered drinking lemon water with Rachel and Delilah one hot day, on that very spot. Delilah . . .

He stopped digging and shoved the iron box in the hole. Then he scooped dirt back on top of the box.

This box is Papa's coffin, Jonathan thought. This shallow hole, his grave. This lonely, secret ceremony is his funeral.

Papa and the cursed pendant will be buried here forever.

Jonathan finished filling the hole and smoothed the dirt. He left nothing to mark the spot.

It is done, Jonathan thought. He stood and wiped the dirt from his hands. That is the end of the horror. The curse is finished. The feud is over.

The Fiers and the Goodes will suffer no more.

Shadyside Village
1900

Nora's entire body tensed as she listened. She held her breath as the footsteps in the hall came closer and closer to her room. She waited for them to stop at her door. . . .

But they passed by.

She exhaled, then picked up her pen and began to write again.

"Jonathan Fier hoped he could bury the curse along with Ezra's ashes," she wrote. "And it seemed to be true. The evil stayed buried for one hundred years. For one hundred years the Goodes and the Fiers lived in peace.

"In fact, the feud was forgotten. Children grew up hearing none of the horrifying stories. They knew nothing of the curse upon the two families."

But it is not easy to end a curse, Nora thought.

Jonathan Fier's great-great granddaughter inno-

cently unleashed the evil once again. During tha
hundred years of sleep, the evil power had grown eve
stronger.

Nora touched the pendant around her neck. Oh, sh
thought mournfully, if only it had stayed burie
forever. . . .

PART THREE

Western Massachusetts 1843

Chapter
19

It is too bad the old apple tree died, thought Elizabeth Fier.

She was kneeling in her green gardening dress, digging with a trowel in the rich dark soil. Heavy leather gloves protected her hands. The apple tree had died, and her brother, Simon, had chopped it down.

Now there was a bare spot in the backyard. Elizabeth thought it looked empty and a bit sad.

But I will take care of that, she thought, adjusting her straw bonnet over her long, dark hair. This flower garden will be even prettier than the old tree. I will fill it with pansies and snapdragons.

As she worked, she hummed a tune her mother had tried to teach her on the piano. She stopped humming as her trowel hit something hard under the dirt. She lifted the trowel out of the dirt, then poked it into the earth again.

There is something buried here, she thought. Maybe some kind of treasure!

A voice inside her head told her it was most likely a root from the old dead tree. But she would soon find out.

She dug around the hard spot, wiping the dirt away with her fingers. She tapped her trowel against it again. It clanged, metal against metal.

A short while later she pulled up a metal box. It had a heavy lock on it, but the box itself was so rusted the hinges had broken.

"Elizabeth!" her mother called from the kitchen door. "Come in and wash up! Supper is ready."

Elizabeth called back, "I will be there in a minute, Mother."

The rusty box fascinated her. What is inside? she wondered. Maybe it really *is* full of treasure.

Carefully she lifted the rusty lid and peered inside. A coarse gray dust covered the bottom of the box. Elizabeth removed her gardening gloves and dipped her fingers into the dust. She touched something solid and pulled it out.

It was a round, silver disk on a silver chain. A silver claw with three talons seemed to clutch the top of the disk. It was studded with four blue stones. On the back Elizabeth saw the inscribed words: *Dominatio per malum.*

Latin, Elizabeth thought. But she did not know what the words meant. Maybe Simon would know.

What an odd necklace, she thought. But I like it.

She stood up, necklace in hand, and ran inside. Her father, Samuel Fier, and her sister and brother, Kate and Simon, were already seated at the dining room table.

It was a warm evening in late spring, but a fire burned in the old brick hearth. The house was very old; it had been in the Fier family for a hundred years. Samuel Fier and his family lived prosperously here.

"Go wash your hands, Elizabeth," said her mother, Katherine. She was a plump, pretty, round-faced woman with light brown hair piled on top of her head.

Elizabeth poured fresh water into the washbasin and rinsed off her hands.

Her mother set a platter of sliced turkey on the table, adding, "I wish you would not stay out in the garden so late, Elizabeth. It leaves you no time to change for supper."

"I am sorry, Mother," Elizabeth replied, returning to the table. She held up the silver disk. "Look what I dug up," she said. "Isn't it strange?"

Kate gave the pendant a dismissive glance and said, "It is ugly."

Kate was seventeen, a year older than Elizabeth. Her hair was a lighter shade of brown and her eyes a lighter shade of blue than Elizabeth's. But they both had the same pale skin and full, red lips.

Their brother, Simon, who was eighteen, had a very tall, thin body with an angular face, thin lips, and black hair. His eyes, too, were black.

Simon studied the pendant as Elizabeth dangled it before him. "Where did you find it?" he asked.

"In the backyard, where I am digging my new garden. It was buried under the old apple tree."

Samuel Fier touched the amulet lightly. "I have never seen anything like it," he said. "I wonder what it was doing buried there. Someone must have buried it for a reason."

"Maybe it should stay buried," Kate joked.

Elizabeth ignored her sister's comment. "I like it," she said. "I am going to wear it as a good-luck charm."

She draped the silver chain around her neck.

Suddenly her neck began to tingle. Elizabeth shuddered and closed her eyes. They burned.

When she opened her eyes, the dining room was gone and she was surrounded by fire!

Hot flames licked at her long curls, at the hem of her dress. Fire singed her eyelashes.

I feel faint, she thought. She shut her eyes again and prepared to be engulfed in flames.

Chapter
20

"Elizabeth! Elizabeth! What is the matter?"

Elizabeth heard the alarmed voices of her mother and father as the flames died away. She shook her head and opened her eyes.

The fire disappeared. The room came into focus, as did the platter of turkey, her family. Everything seemed normal.

"Elizabeth, what happened?" her mother asked.

Elizabeth groped for a chair and sat down. "It is nothing, Mother, really," she said. The flames were already fading from her memory. "I just felt faint for a minute. I am all right now."

"You need something to eat," said Mrs. Fier.

"You are probably right," said Elizabeth. "I am very hungry."

For the rest of the evening Elizabeth felt fine. There

were no other strange incidents. Soon she forgot all about the frightening sensation of fire.

A few weeks later the flowers in Elizabeth's garden were beginning to sprout. As for the strange pendant she had found there, it was now her favorite piece of jewelry. She never took it off.

The Fiers were sitting down to supper on a warm June evening. Elizabeth was just passing a dish of fresh peas to Simon.

Suddenly they heard a knock on the door.

"Who could that be?" asked Mrs. Fier, filling their glasses with water.

"I will answer it," said Elizabeth. She stood up and hurried to the door.

There, in the fading light, stood a tall, ragged man. The sight of him startled Elizabeth.

His broad-brimmed straw hat was caked with dirt and sat low over his gaunt face. His black jacket and trousers were faded and hung loose on his skeletal frame. His boots were worn thin.

His eyes, hard and glittering, stared at the disk around Elizabeth's neck, but he said nothing.

He must be a poor drifter, Elizabeth said to herself, collecting her thoughts. But why does he not speak?

"What do you want?" she asked him.

He raised his eyes from the pendant to Elizabeth's face. Then he moved his cracked lips. "Please help me," he pleaded in a weak voice. "I am hungry. Can you spare any food or water?"

As Elizabeth glanced back at her family's bountiful supper, the drifter added, "I will gladly do a day's work in return for a meal."

Mr. Fier came to the door and stood behind his

daughter. "Please come in," he said to the drifter. "We were just sitting down to eat, and we have plenty to share."

"Thank you, sir," said the drifter. He smiled through his dry lips and stepped inside.

Elizabeth watched him sit down and take a plate of food. His hands are bony, she thought with pity. And he looks sick. That must be what makes his eyes glitter so. The poor man!

First the drifter drank two full glasses of water. Then he began to eat, rapidly shoveling the food into his mouth.

He said nothing until he had eaten every morsel on his plate. Elizabeth struggled not to stare at him as he gobbled up his food.

When he had finished the first serving, Mrs. Fier took his plate and refilled it. The man thanked her very sincerely.

"My name is Franklin," he told them. "But my friends call me Frank. I consider you all my friends now."

All the Fiers smiled.

Now that he has eaten a bit, Elizabeth thought, his eyes are warmer and his face is friendlier. To think that I was frightened of a sick, weak, hungry man!

"Do you live around here, Frank?" asked Mr. Fier.

Frank shook his head. "I have no home," he said. "Not anymore."

There was silence for a moment as Frank tore at a slice of bread with his teeth.

"I used to have a family," he continued. "I was one of seven brothers. We lived on a farm with my mother and father. But I lost them all, my whole family, and the farm, too. I am alone in the world now."

He spread a thick layer of honey on the bread.

"Now I roam around, picking up work where I can find it. But sometimes there is no work to be had. And when there is no work, there is no food."

"Why don't you settle down somewhere?" Mrs. Fier asked.

"I would, ma'am," Frank said. "I certainly would. I would settle down anywhere on earth, if I had a good reason to."

His lifted his gaze from his plate. Elizabeth felt a little shiver.

He is looking right at me, she thought.

Frank wiped his mouth and pushed his chair back from the table. "That was a delicious supper," he said, standing up. "I thank you very kindly for it. Now I feel ready to do just about anything. You name the task, and I will do it for you."

"Oh, no, Frank," Mrs. Fier protested. "We would not think of making you work for your supper. We were glad we could help."

"Nevertheless, ma'am," Frank said. "I would feel better if I could do something for you."

"We do not need anything done," said Simon. "But you could use a good hot bath, I bet."

"Oh, no," said Frank. "I could not trouble you."

But the Fiers insisted, and Frank had to accept. While their mother cleaned up the supper dishes, Kate and Elizabeth got the wooden bathtub out of the pantry and set it on the kitchen floor. They boiled water and poured it into the tub.

Then the women left the room so Frank could take a bath. Simon left a clean suit of clothes for him on a chair.

Elizabeth paused at the door on her way out of the

kitchen. She turned around just as Frank was taking off his dirty, tattered shirt. The movement of his arms made the muscles ripple through his back.

Embarrassed, Elizabeth hurried out. She hoped Frank did not know that she had had a glimpse of his bare back. It was not a proper sight for a young lady.

All the Fiers waited for Frank by the fire in the parlor. Kate bent over her needlepoint, and Elizabeth worked at her knitting. Kate's birthday was coming up, and Elizabeth had decided to knit a scarf for her.

Elizabeth glanced up, startled by a noise at the parlor door.

There stood Frank, fresh from his bath. Elizabeth had to stop herself from gasping out loud at the change in him.

She realized that he was probably ten years younger than she had thought at first, closer to twenty than thirty. His face had taken on a new warmth, now that he was clean, fed, and rested. His hair was neatly combed, and Simon's borrowed clothes fit him elegantly.

He is handsome, Elizabeth realized. Very handsome.

She suddenly became aware of the weight of the amulet hanging from her neck, and the coolness of the metal against her skin. She held it in her palm, and it grew warm.

Frank says he is just a drifter, Elizabeth thought as she watched him take a seat by the fire. But there is more to him than that. He did not tell us much about his family, or say where he comes from. Who is he, really?

She would soon find out.

* * *

Frank leaned back against the cushioned chair by the fireplace, grinning at the Fier family gathered around him.

They are all smiling at me, he thought. They are so welcoming to the poor, starving drifter into their home. They are being so kind, so good-hearted.

They will take me in, he mused, and they will nurse me back to health. As I get stronger, I will help them out around the house, entertain their sweet daughters and their lonely son.

Soon they will begin to trust me, and before they know it, depend upon me. They will all love me, all five of them, like a brother and like a son.

Frank warmed his hands over the crackling flames in the hearth. Mrs. Fier offered him a cup of hot coffee.

It is beginning already, he thought. I can see the warmth shining in their eyes. They want to help me. They are beginning to love me.

I will wait. I will wait until they all love me as much as they love one another. I will wait and endure it all.

Then I will turn on them—and that will make it all worthwhile. I will enjoy the shock and terror in their faces. It will make up for everything my family suffered at their hands and all the pain I have endured to find them.

I, Franklin—the last of the Goodes.

Chapter
21

Frank finished his coffee. Then he stood up, stretched, and smiled at the Fiers.

"Thank you all, for everything," he said. "You were very kind. But you must be getting tired, and I am keeping you up. I will be moving on now, so you can go to sleep."

"You are leaving?" said Kate.

Oh, no, Elizabeth thought. He cannot leave. Not yet.

"I have imposed on your hospitality long enough," Frank said modestly. "You had better be careful—if you are too kind, you will have ragged drifters like Franklin Goode at your door every night!"

Mr. Fier chuckled at that. He put a hand on Frank's shoulder and said, "We cannot let you go off into the night this way. You must spend the night here, with us. I insist."

"Please, Frank," said Mrs. Fier. "I will not get a wink of sleep if you leave now. I will worry about you all night."

"Well . . ." said Frank, pretending to think it over. "I would not want to interfere with your sleep, Mrs. Fier. I will be glad to stay. But just for tonight. Then I will be on my way."

Hurray, Elizabeth thought to herself, secretly. He is staying!

Mrs. Fier sent Elizabeth to get the guest room ready.

He is so brave, Elizabeth thought as she tucked a fresh linen sheet under the pillow. He is strong and self-reliant.

She paused, remembering the ripple of muscle she had seen on his back. The memory gave her goose bumps.

Franklin Goode, she thought. And then—she could not help herself—"Mrs. Franklin Goode." She turned the sound of it over in her mind.

It is a nice name, Elizabeth thought. A very nice name indeed.

Elizabeth heard the heavy blows of an ax in the backyard as she made her way to the kitchen window to peer out.

There was Frank, wearing Simon's work clothes, chopping wood. When he raised the ax above his head, the metal glinted in the sun.

It is a warm day, Elizabeth thought. Frank must be very thirsty. So she poured a glass of cool water and took it to him.

Frank smiled at the sight of her. He gave the log one

last blow, then set down the ax. He took the glass from Elizabeth's hand and drank down the water without a word.

Then he returned the empty glass to her, saying, "Thank you very much, Elizabeth. You must have read my mind."

"I just thought you might be thirsty, that is all," she replied.

Frank sat down on the pile of logs and gazed up into Elizabeth's face. She found herself blushing.

"Have you ever seen the sea, Elizabeth?" he asked.

She shook her head. "I have never been out of this town. Well, I have been to Worcester once or twice—"

"Someday soon, Elizabeth, you must see the ocean. If you have not seen it yourself, you cannot imagine it. It is so wild, and so beautiful. On a clear day the ocean is a dark blue-green color that is so hard to describe. But—your eyes—"

He stared intently at her face. Elizabeth's eyes were locked onto his. His gaze was hypnotic.

"But what?" she asked him. "What about my eyes?"

"Your eyes," Frank said. "Your eyes are the only thing I have ever seen that are the same wild color as the ocean."

Elizabeth's heart fluttered. She had never heard anyone speak that way before.

It is as if he is speaking directly through his heart, she thought.

"I am just about finished chopping wood," Frank said. "I would like to take a walk to look around. Would you do me the honor of accompanying me, Elizabeth?"

"I would love to," she replied. "Though I warn you,

you will be disappointed. There is not much to see in town."

"I am not interested in towns anyway," said Frank. "I would rather take a walk through the woods."

She set the glass on top of a log. He offered her his arm, and she accepted it. They walked across the grass of the back lawn to the woods that stood at the edge of the Fier property.

The woods were magical that day. Rays of sunlight streamed through the tall pine trees, and the brown needles made a soft, fragrant carpet on the ground. Elizabeth led Frank to a clearing where two large, flat stones sat side by side like chairs.

"Kate and Simon and I loved to play here when we were children," she explained. "We used to pretend this clearing was the throne room in a castle. Simon sat on that big stone there, and Kate on the smaller one."

She sat down on the smaller rock, leaving the larger one to Frank. "Simon was the king, and Kate was the queen. I usually had to be the princess."

Frank smiled and sat down on his rock. Elizabeth paused and listened. She heard only the rustling of the squirrels and the chirping of the birds. There were no people around, she felt sure.

Still, she lowered her voice as she said, "There is an old woman who lives in these woods. She hobbles through the pines with a cane, all stooped over. She has white hair and wears black clothes. Simon and Kate and I used to see her when we played in this very spot. We ran if we saw her coming."

"Why?"

Elizabeth shrugged, feeling slightly silly. "All the

children were afraid of her. We called her Old Aggie. People said she was a witch."

"I am sure they were just trying to frighten you," said Frank. "Your parents were probably hoping a story like that would keep you from wandering too far off."

Elizabeth smiled. "I suppose you are right. Still, I always believed that Old Aggie really was a witch. One boy I knew said that if you got close enough, Aggie's cane turned into a live snake."

Elizabeth could not stop herself from shivering. "I often wonder if she is still alive."

"I am sure she is not," Frank said in a comforting voice. She smiled. She felt safe with him there.

A ray of sunlight fell on the silver pendant around Elizabeth's neck. Frank reached for it.

"Where did you get this necklace?" he asked.

"It is a strange piece of jewelry, is it not?" said Elizabeth. "I found it in our backyard. It was buried in a rusty old strongbox."

Frank studied the pendant, turning it over in his hand, rubbing his fingers over the blue jewels. "What do the words mean?" he asked her. "Do you know who it belonged to?"

Elizabeth shook her head. "I do not know anything about it. But I like it. I wear it for good luck."

Frank nodded absently and studied the amulet for another long minute. Elizabeth found it odd that he was so interested in her charm.

Frank seemed to read her thoughts. He let the amulet fall back against her chest and smiled at her.

"I am curious about it," he said, indicating the amulet, "because it belongs to you. I only hope that this good-luck charm has enough power to keep you safe. Someday you might need a real protector. The world is full of danger, Elizabeth."

His eyes were shining as he said this, and Elizabeth's heart swelled at his words.

He is talking about himself, she thought happily. He wants to protect me. Could it be true? Could he really be falling in love with me?

They strolled silently back to the house, arm in arm. Occasionally Elizabeth glanced at his face and found him watching her, a warm smile lighting up his face.

"That dog followed me all the way to Boston!" Frank said, and all the Fiers laughed. Elizabeth and her family were sitting around the supper table while Frank told them about his adventures. Elizabeth watched the rapt faces of her parents as they listened to Frank's stories.

They like him, she thought happily. She wanted them to approve of him. She had an idea in the back of her mind that they wanted her to marry someone with property and money—and Frank was penniless.

But character is more important than money, Elizabeth told herself. Surely Mother and Father can see that.

"You are not much older than I am," Simon said wistfully, "but you have seen and done so much."

Simon envies him, Elizabeth thought, suppressing a smile. She could not help being pleased at seeing her older brother humbled a bit. As the eldest Fier and the only boy, Simon sometimes acted as if he were a prince.

"Do not envy me, Simon," Frank said. "If I still had

a wonderful family like yours, I would never have left home."

Frank's eyes paused on Elizabeth, and she smiled at him.

"What exactly happened to your family, Frank?" Mrs. Fier asked. "You have not told us."

Frank set his fork and knife on his plate and wiped his mouth with his napkin. The Fiers watched him, waiting to hear the tragic story he would tell.

"My family died mysteriously," Frank began. "One by one. First my parents, then each of my brothers, until only I, the youngest, was left. They showed no sign of sickness, just died very suddenly, one at a time."

Mrs. Fier clucked her tongue, and Mr. Fier slowly shook his head.

"Each time someone died we called the doctor, but he never knew what had happened. No one understood it. All doctors were at a complete loss."

Frank paused and took a breath. "At any rate, the day came when I was the last Goode left. I was twelve years old. No one wanted to take me in, for fear they would catch whatever it was my family had. So I went off on my own. To this day, I wonder why I alone was spared. I am still waiting for the curse to come and strike me dead."

Elizabeth felt her eyes fill with tears. My poor Frank, she thought. She wished she could reach across the table to comfort him, but she knew her mother would think her too forward.

She glanced at her sister Kate. Kate's eyes, too, were shining with tears. Her face glowed as she listened to Frank, hanging on his every word.

Kate's expression made Elizabeth suddenly feel uncomfortable. Why was Kate gazing at Frank that way?

Elizabeth did not want to think about it, so she turned away. Soon she forgot about it, caught up in the story of Frank's first night alone.

After supper the family gathered in the parlor. Mrs. Fier sat at the piano and played. Simon and Frank began a game of chess. Elizabeth picked up her knitting needles, and Kate focused on her needlepoint.

The fire crackled and sputtered; the gaslights hissed; the clock ticked on the mantel.

Elizabeth could not concentrate on the scarf she was knitting. She glanced over at Simon and Frank to be sure they were not paying attention to her. Then she leaned across the couch toward Kate.

"I like Frank very much," she confided to her sister in a whisper. "Don't you?"

Kate glanced up from her work, her eyes startled and wide. Her hands fidgeted nervously.

"Of course I like him," she whispered back. "We all do. Why are you asking me this?"

"I was just making conversation," whispered Elizabeth.

Kate seemed to be embarrassed as if she had been caught in a lie. She put down her needlepoint and left the room, her full skirts rustling as she walked.

Frank glanced up from the chess game when Kate left the room. He forced himself not to look at Elizabeth. Instead, he turned his head toward the fire so she would not see the smirk on his face.

This is going to be easier than I imagined, he thought with satisfaction.

"Your move, Frank," said Simon.

Frank tried to concentrate on the game. He could not let Simon beat him, not the first game. He would let Simon take the third one, maybe.

Simon was staring at the chess pieces with total concentration. A lock of black hair hung over his forehead.

He is just a boy, Frank thought. He does not understand what is happening.

My plan is working, Simon, Frank told him in his mind. Your family likes me better with every passing day. Even you enjoy my company, do you not, Simon?

I am winning your trust, all of you. Soon you will believe anything I say.

As soon as I have that perfect trust, I will act.

I watched my brothers die, one by one. You will soon know what that feels like, Simon.

I will become your sisters' only hope. Then I will watch them die, one by one.

Frank slid his queen across the board. "Checkmate," he said, grinning.

Chapter 22

"Put that watering can down."

Elizabeth glanced up from her garden, startled by the sound of a deep, booming voice. Then she broke into a laugh. It was only Frank, teasing her.

"It has not rained all week," she protested. "My flowers are thirsty." She straightened her straw bonnet and continued watering the garden.

Frank stepped closer to her. "All right, water them," he teased. "I will go for a walk in the woods by myself."

She pouted. "I am almost finished. There." She set the watering can down. "Let me come with you. I would not want you to get lost."

She took off her sunbonnet and left it on the grass. Her hair was tied back with a red satin ribbon. Frank took her hand and they started off through the woods.

Every day, when the weather was fair, Frank and Elizabeth walked through the woods to the clearing with the two flat rocks. Elizabeth looked forward to their walks more and more. No one else in the family knew about them.

I am not keeping our walks a secret, exactly, Elizabeth thought. I just have not mentioned them.

Elizabeth knew that her mother would want to come on the walks—but that would ruin them. They would not be the same with her mother—not at all.

Anyway, Frank has never done anything improper, she thought. I have no reason to worry.

Now they had reached the clearing. Elizabeth sat down on her rock, the smaller one. But instead of sitting on his rock, Frank lingered behind her.

Elizabeth felt a gentle tug on her hair, and then felt it fall loose about her shoulders. She sighed. Frank had untied the ribbon from her hair.

She leaned back against him. Frank playfully draped the red ribbon across her throat. She giggled. He tugged on it lightly. She giggled again.

Then Elizabeth sat still, quivering with excitement, waiting to see what would happen next.

Behind her, just out of her sight, Frank held the two ends of the ribbon in his hands.

He wound each end around his index fingers.

Elizabeth sat in front of him, trusting her fate to him, completely in his power.

He smiled.

Then he tugged on the ribbon, preparing to strangle her.

Chapter
23

A twig cracked nearby. Frank froze.

Elizabeth's body tensed.

She heard the snap of another twig. Then the shuffle of someone moving through pine needles.

Someone was close by.

The ribbon fell from Frank's hand.

Elizabeth climbed to her feet and clutched at his arm, her eyes scanning the woods.

The shuffling noise moved closer. Then Elizabeth saw a stooped figure walking slowly and steadily their way.

A white-haired old woman, dressed all in black, hobbled through the pine needles, a cane poking the ground in front of her.

Elizabeth gasped. "Aggie!"

She grabbed Frank's hand and pulled him through the woods, back toward the house. She did not look back, and she did not stop until they were safely in her yard.

"That was the old woman," Elizabeth said, panting. "Old Aggie. She is still alive!"

"She appeared to be a harmless old woman," Frank told her.

"No, she is not!" Elizabeth cried breathlessly. "Somehow I know she is *not* just a harmless old woman. There is something different about her . . ."

Frank took Elizabeth in his arms and held her tight. She closed her eyes and rested her head against his chest, catching her breath.

She felt safe now. I will always feel safe with Frank, she thought.

Calm at last, she lifted her head and smiled. "It is too bad Old Aggie came along," she whispered. "She spoiled such a lovely afternoon."

Frank hesitated a second, then smiled.

He is embarrassed, Elizabeth thought fondly. He was going to kiss me. He was going to ask me to marry him, and he wanted to surprise me. But now he knows that I know.

Oh, well, she thought as she and Frank started back toward the house. He will ask me soon. And I will not disappoint him. I plan to say yes.

Elizabeth opened the back door, and she and Frank stepped into the kitchen. They found Kate stirring a pot of soup.

Kate glanced at her sister and Frank when they walked in. Elizabeth smiled at her and said, "How is the soup coming?"

Kate did not answer. Her mouth fell open, but no sound came out. She dropped the soup spoon and ran from the room.

123

Elizabeth stared after her, shocked. She suddenly felt aware of her hair hanging loose about her shoulders. She turned to Frank, who had a strange, thoughtful expression on his face.

"What could be the matter?" Elizabeth asked him. "Do you think Kate is all right?"

"I am sure she is fine," Frank replied. "Perhaps she burned her hand on the pot."

"I had better make sure she is not hurt," said Elizabeth. She started to follow Kate, but Frank caught her by the wrist and held her back.

"Do not worry about her," he said. "Your mother is upstairs. I am sure she is taking care of Kate."

"I suppose you are right," Elizabeth said doubtfully. She felt she should go after her sister, but Frank seemed to want her to stay with him.

The soup began to boil. Elizabeth picked up the spoon to stir it.

I cannot go running after Kate, she reasoned as she felt Frank run his hand through her hair. Someone has to stay here to watch the soup, after all. If it boils over, we will not have any supper tonight, and I am sure Kate does not want that.

A few weeks later Elizabeth paced the house impatiently, searching for Frank.

Where *is* he? she wondered. It was time for their walk, and she could not find him anywhere. She sighed and sat down on a chair in the parlor and picked up her knitting.

I might as well work on Kate's scarf while I am waiting for him, she thought. I might as well make myself useful, as Mother would say.

The back door slammed. Here he is at last, she thought.

She stood up, waiting to greet him. But it was not Frank who burst in to the parlor. It was Kate.

Kate's face was flushed, and she carried a basket of mulberries in her arms.

"Oh, Elizabeth!" she cried, letting the basket fall to the floor. She ran to her sister and threw her arms around her neck. "The most wonderful thing has happened!"

"What on earth is it?" asked Elizabeth. She had never seen Kate so excited.

"You will be so happy for me!" Kate gushed. She took Elizabeth's hands in hers, knitting and all, and danced her around the room. "Mother will play the organ, and you can decorate the cake!"

"The cake?" asked Elizabeth. "Kate, what are you *talking* about?"

"Haven't you guessed by now?" cried Kate. "Frank and I are going to be married!"

Chapter 24

"Married!" Elizabeth uttered, unable to hide her shock. "You—and Frank?"

"What is all the commotion in there?" Simon and Mr. Fier came hurrying in from the front porch, and Mrs. Fier appeared on the stairs. "What is going on, girls?"

Elizabeth stood frozen in place, trying to stop her knees from shaking, while she watched Kate run into their mother's arms. "Mother! Frank has asked me to marry him!"

Elizabeth stood aside to watch the happy uproar that followed this announcement. Mrs. Fier's kind face lit up, and Mr. Fier clapped his hands delightedly.

Finally Elizabeth could not help herself. She could not keep the words from bursting from her lips. "It cannot be!" she cried in a trembling voice. "Frank loves *me!*"

No one seemed to hear her.

Simon asked, "Where is Frank? I want to congratulate him."

How can this be? thought Elizabeth. Is this really happening? Kate and Frank?

She wanted to scream. She wanted to fly out of the room. She wanted to disappear forever.

How can this be? *How can this be?*

She uttered a sob of grief, of anger, of disbelief.

Kate and Frank?

Elizabeth remembered just then all the times that Kate had acted strangely around her and Frank. When Elizabeth told Kate that she liked Frank, and when Elizabeth and Frank had come in from the woods and found Kate stirring soup. Kate had seemed upset those times. Now it all made sense.

Kate had loved Frank all along.

And Kate had *stolen* Frank from her!

"How *could* you?" Elizabeth shrieked at the top of her lungs.

Her new outburst made everyone fall silent, and they all turned to stare at Elizabeth.

"How *could* you?" she raged at Kate again. "My own sister!"

"What?" Kate gaped at her, bewildered. "Lizzie—what are you talking about?"

"I—I—I—"

Elizabeth found herself speechless now.

Afraid of the intense anger she felt, afraid she might explode from rage, she tightened her fists around the knitting needles and ran from the room.

I must find Frank! I must find Frank! she told herself as violent sobs escaped from her throat.

She pushed blindly through the kitchen, out the

back door, and into the woods. Behind her, she could hear Kate calling her name.

Elizabeth ignored her. Frank was all that mattered. Kate could not be trusted.

"Frank!" she screamed. "Frank!"

Her feet padded over the brown carpet of pine needles. Sharp branches tore at her skirt, but she barely noticed.

Elizabeth had almost reached the clearing when she realized she was still clutching Kate's unfinished scarf and her knitting needles. She tossed them onto the ground and kept running.

"Frank!" she called.

Far behind her, she could still hear Kate's worried call: "Elizabeth! Elizabeth!"

Simon and his parents were left standing in the parlor in a daze. None of them understood what had just happened.

Wasn't Kate's announcement a joyful one?

At last Mrs. Fier said, "Simon, run after the girls and see what this is all about."

Simon nodded and started after his sisters. He heard voices ringing through the woods. They were his sisters' voices.

No sign of Frank. Simon could not help wondering where Frank was all this time.

He tried to follow the voices, but they seemed to come from all directions in the thick woods, like birdcalls.

Then, suddenly, there was a bloodcurdling scream. Simon froze. The woods fell silent.

Silent as death.

What was that? Where had it come from?

He ran in the direction of the scream. Soon he found himself in a clearing. He recognized it as the place where he and his sisters had played as children.

Simon's eyes frantically searched the clearing.

Who screamed? Why?

Behind the bigger of the two rocks he saw something dark. Simon squinted hard until it came into focus.

A pair of dainty black high-button boots.

He took a step closer, his heart beating wildly. The ground seemed to tilt under him.

Taking a deep breath, Simon peered behind the rock.

"Ohh." He gripped the top of the rock as his eyes landed on Kate's body. She lay sprawled on her back, her light brown hair spread out around her head like a halo. Her pale blue eyes were open, reflecting the sky.

Simon gripped the rock till his hand hurt. "Kate?"

She did not answer. She stared up lifelessly, a knitting needle plunged through her heart.

Chapter
25

Elizabeth sat in the rocking chair by the fireplace. Her hair fell in tangles down her back. Her eyes, red-rimmed and bloodshot, stared out from her tear-stained face. She rocked back and forth, back and forth, hugging her knees under her torn blue dress.

"Kate was a liar," Elizabeth murmured, rocking. "Kate was a liar. Kate was a liar."

Mrs. Fier stood over the rocking chair, helplessly wringing her hands. Mr. Fier stared at his daughter in horror and disbelief.

Frank sat tensely on the couch, his eyes darting from face to face. Simon paced the room, lost in his own unhappy thoughts, not seeing anyone.

"Kate was a liar," Elizabeth murmured. "Frank did not love Kate. Frank loves Elizabeth."

She lifted her head to search for Frank. Her eyes met the horrified stares of her parents instead.

"Why are you staring at me that way!" she screamed. "I did not kill her! I swear it!"

Her mother and father said nothing. Elizabeth rocked again.

They do not believe me, she thought bitterly. It is written all over their faces. They think I killed my own sister. They think I stabbed Kate with a knitting needle.

Frank was at her side now, kneeling beside the rocking chair. He took her warm, sticky hand in his. His hands were so cool, so calm and soothing.

"Elizabeth is the gentlest creature I know," Frank said to her parents. "She could never kill anyone."

Still her parents said nothing. Her mother's face was twisted in grief, fear, and confusion.

Elizabeth focused on Frank only.

Frank's handsome face was calming. He gave her a tiny, encouraging smile. At once she felt better.

I would be all alone in the world without Frank, she thought.

Then she said to her family, "Frank believes in me. He knows I am innocent. Why don't *you* believe me?"

No one said a word, but Elizabeth could see it on their faces. They blame me for Kate's death, she thought. They blame me *and* Frank.

Mr. Fier stormed out of the room. Mrs. Fier hurried after him. Then Simon, too, strode out, disgust registered on his face.

Elizabeth dissolved into tears and continued to rock back and forth, back and forth, crying.

"Hush," Frank whispered. "Hush, Elizabeth. Forget about them. There is nothing you can do to make them believe you."

He gave her a white handkerchief. She dried her eyes. "My own family," she whispered. "They will never believe in me. They will never speak to me again, I suppose."

"You are too hard on them," Frank said. "They do not want to accept the truth. They *cannot* accept it. That is why they will not believe you."

Now he took both of her hands in his. "But I believe in you, Elizabeth. I always will."

She stopped rocking and smiled at him gratefully.

"It is hard for a mother and father to imagine their own child killing herself," Frank went on. "But I know that is what happened. Kate killed herself. Your parents did not see it, Simon did not see it, but you and I could see it. Kate was going mad."

Elizabeth nodded. All that strange behavior. It was the only logical explanation.

"Kate was jealous of you," Frank said. "You know I never told Kate I would marry her. How could I? I am in love with you."

He kissed her hands. Elizabeth drank in every word he said.

"Kate made it up," said Frank. "She made up that whole story about our engagement. She ran right to you to tell you first. I think she really believed it was true. She was mad, truly mad, the poor girl."

"Poor Kate," Elizabeth whispered.

"She was capable of anything," said Frank. "No one could help her."

Elizabeth knew he was right. She sighed and started rocking again. "Frank, I cannot stay here. They all hate me." She gestured toward the second floor, where her parents and Simon had gone. "I must get away."

"I know what to do," Frank said. "We can run away together. We shall elope."

He gently took her chin in his hand and turned her face toward his. "Elizabeth Fier, will you marry me?"

They were the most wonderful words Elizabeth had ever heard. She felt a little of her old spirit come back.

"Yes," she said, throwing her arms around Frank's neck. "Yes. We will leave tonight."

Elizabeth's touch gave Frank a cold chill, but he did not let it show.

Yes, he thought to himself. We shall elope. We shall leave this house tonight, Elizabeth and I.

But only one of us will return. And it will not be Elizabeth.

This trusting girl will pack up all her belongings, he thought gleefully, and follow me wherever I go. I will take her into the woods to kill her, just as I killed her sister.

Kate's face was so wonderfully surprised at the end, he thought. When she saw me coming, she smiled. She opened her arms to me. Even when I raised the knitting needle over my head, she did not understand. She had no idea what was happening—not until the very last second.

Then she understood it all. It came to her in a flash.

The horror of betrayal.

The Fiers need to learn what that feels like. They will all know soon enough.

Chapter
26

Simon paced the house as if in a daze, weighted down with grief and sadness, his mind whirring with thoughts of Kate's death.

His parents were locked in their room. Through the door he could hear his father's heavy boots on the floor, his mother weeping and wailing for her daughters.

Elizabeth, too, was shut in her room. Simon put his ear to her door. He heard her scurrying around.

What could she be doing? he wondered. He was afraid she had lost her mind.

Evening fell. No one prepared supper; no one thought of eating. Simon's grief gave way to uneasy restlessness.

I *have* to get out of this house, he thought, or I will go mad!

The sky was still hovering over the trees as Simon

made his way out of the house, but once in the woods the darkness surprised him. It was midsummer, and the leaves were at their thickest. They blocked out most all of the fading sunlight.

Simon found the woods unusually still. The daytime animals had already hidden away for the night. The nocturnal creatures had not yet crept out of their dens to hunt.

Simon walked on, deeper and deeper into the woods. All he wanted was to put his house and family behind him.

He found himself at the clearing with the two flat stones. The woods were almost completely dark now. Simon sat on the bigger stone, the one that had once been his throne. He patted the smaller stone beside it. That had been Kate's.

Kate was dead now.

Kate is dead.

He realized he could not escape from his grief.

Simon peered through the darkness, staring at the spot where he had found Kate's body. A cold chill ran down his back as the ugly sight returned to him: Kate's eyes, so glassy, so empty. The needle poking out of her chest. The blood had spread across the front of her dress.

The blood had spread like evil, Simon thought. And now there is evil everywhere. It lives inside my family's house, right now. Evil lives inside Elizabeth and Frank. It lives in these woods, in the air around me.

He took a big gulp of air, then exhaled.

It lives inside me, too, he thought. I feel it. There is evil living inside me.

Then the deep silence of the woods was broken. Simon heard a noise. The snap of a twig, somewhere nearby.

Simon froze. He listened.

Was it an animal? A deer?

Snap. The noise was behind him.

How had it moved so quickly, so quietly?

Simon wanted to turn, to look. But he was paralyzed with fear.

Something grabbed him from behind.

A claw!

Pain shot through his shoulder. The claw dug deeper.

Simon turned at last. He took one look at his attacker, and the blood drained from his face. He screamed.

Chapter
27

Old Aggie!

Simon felt the blood throb at his temples. He had never seen the old woman so close up.

Her face was hidden by a black hood. In one wrinkled hand she held the cane she always carried. The fingers of the other hand were covered with rings. They dug into Simon's shoulder. Aggie was so stooped that her head was even with Simon's as he sat before her.

Simon tried to stand.

But with one wrinkled hand, the old woman held him in place. The pain in Simon's shoulder deepened.

"Do not go," she commanded in a gravelly voice.

Shaking, Simon tried to calm down. It is only an old woman, he told himself. Only an old woman.

"S-sorry I screamed like that. You startled me," he stammered.

Old Aggie slowly let go of his shoulder. Simon felt her long fingernails pull out of his skin.

She held out her bony, jeweled hand. "Give me your hand," she croaked.

Simon hesitated. He saw her black eyes glowing like coal under her hood.

"Your hand," she repeated in her deep, raspy voice.

Simon obeyed. He offered her his trembling hand.

She took it firmly in her own and bent close to his palm, her long, crooked nose almost grazing his hand.

Finally she released his hand and trained her eyes on his face. Simon's heart pounded as he waited to see what would happen next.

The children said she would kill us and eat our hearts, he thought, remembering his childhood fears of Old Aggie.

But that had to be a foolish childhood tale.

Aggie cleared her throat. "Hear me, Simon Fier, and hear me well."

How does she know my name? Simon wondered. He did not dare to ask her.

"You have allowed a man named Franklin Goode into your home. Am I right?" croaked Old Aggie.

Simon nodded.

"That was foolish of you. He will destroy you all. You must stop him."

Simon swallowed.

Old Aggie continued. "Franklin Goode killed your sister Kate. At this very moment he plots the death of Elizabeth."

Simon was shaken. Could the old woman be speaking the truth?

"Fier," Old Aggie murmured. "Fier. Fier. A terrible name. A cursed name."

"What do you mean?" Simon demanded. "Why do you say that, old woman?"

"Your fate lies in your name," Old Aggie replied, her face hidden in the darkness of her hood. "The letters in your name—they can be rearranged to spell *fire*. Fier. Fire. Fier. Fire." She repeated the two words several times in her croaking voice, chanting them to sound like curses.

"I do not understand," Simon confessed.

"That is how your family will come to its end," Old Aggie rasped.

"What? How?" he demanded. "How?"

"By fire," she murmured. "Fier. Fire. You shall meet your end by fire."

Simon gasped as Old Aggie pointed a long, terrible finger into his face. "You are under a curse!" she cried. "A curse cast by the Goodes, and by your own evil history. Now you have allowed a Goode into your home, into your family. Your suffering will know no end, Simon Fier."

"But wh-what can I do?" Simon choked out in a shrill, tight voice. "What?"

The old woman reached into the folds of her long black robe and pulled out a small silver dagger, its handle studded with dark rubies.

"Take this dagger," she whispered. "Its tip is poisoned. You have only to scratch the skin of your enemy with it, and he will die."

Simon took the dagger from her with a trembling hand.

"Be careful," she warned him. "The dagger will only work once. Do not waste the poison."

"I—I will not," Simon promised, gazing at the dagger as if it were alive.

Old Aggie nodded. "Go now. Hurry, before it is too late."

Simon jumped up and began to run through the dark woods.

When he glanced back at the clearing, the old woman had disappeared.

Had she told him the truth?

Was the rest of his family in danger? In danger from Frank Goode?

Or was the old woman as crazy as the children always claimed?

A yellow glow led him back to his house. He emerged from the woods and saw the kitchen ablaze with light. The rest of the house was in darkness.

Simon burst into the kitchen doorway and stopped.

He stared down and saw his mother sprawled in a dark puddle of blood on the floor.

Simon's father was slumped over the kitchen table. Bright red blood had flowed from a wound in his side and lay pooled on the floor.

"Simon!"

Elizabeth's voice.

Simon raised his eyes from the horrifying sight of his murdered parents.

Elizabeth was cowering in a corner by the hearth. Frank Goode stood before her, an ax raised over her head.

The ax that he had used to murder Simon's parents.

The blade was stained blood-red in the firelight.

Simon cried out as Frank let the ax fall.

Chapter
28

Simon tried to cry out, but the sound caught in his throat.

Elizabeth uttered a high-pitched howl.

The ax blade made a whistling, slicing sound as it fell.

It grazed Elizabeth's head, chopping off a clump of her hair.

As she began to sob, Frank tossed his head back and laughed.

"Just teasing you, Elizabeth," he said. "But the next one is for real."

Elizabeth pressed herself against the wall and panted. Without realizing it, she had wrapped her hand around the pendant she had found in the garden.

Frank turned to Simon and smiled.

"The Fiers nearly won," he said. "Your family nearly managed to destroy the Goodes forever. That is what your ancestors wanted, is it not? To wipe us from the face of the earth?"

Gripped with the horror of the scene he had walked in on, Simon struggled to breathe. The last trickles of his father's blood onto the floor roared like a rushing waterfall in Simon's ears.

Frank took a step toward him.

"In the end, though," Frank continued slowly, calmly, "the Goodes will survive. I am the last of my family—but that is enough. I have served my ancestors well. I have lived to destroy the Fiers."

He took another step toward Simon, the ax blade red and gleaming in the firelight.

Simon's trembling hand squeezed the handle of the silver dagger, hidden under his coat. He hoped Old Aggie had been telling the truth about the dagger's power.

Frank hoisted the ax high. With a loud grunt, he swung the ax down toward Simon's head.

Elizabeth's scream pierced the air.

Simon ducked out of the way as the ax blade dug deeply into the tabletop.

Simon had the advantage and drew the dagger from under his coat, lunged forward, and scratched the blade across Frank's arm.

A tiny red line, as thin as a hair, appeared along Frank's forearm. He stared at it, then at Simon. He burst out laughing.

"Is that how you hope to stop me, Simon?" he cried. "With a scratch from a dagger?"

Simon stood panting, his chest heaving.

Frank laughed.

With every sound Frank uttered, Simon felt his

heart grow colder. He raged with hate for Frank and for every Goode who had ever lived.

Frank turned back to Elizabeth. "If you are going to fight me, Simon, I will have to take care of your little sister first," he said.

Elizabeth had darted away from the corner. But there was nowhere for her to run.

Frank easily pulled the ax blade from the tabletop and took a step toward Elizabeth. Then another.

"Simon—*help me!*" Elizabeth cried. *"Help me!"*

Frank took another step toward her. He started to raise the ax.

The old woman's magic—it hadn't worked! Simon realized.

I am not strong enough to pull the ax from Frank's grip. I am not strong enough to fight him.

I foolishly counted on Old Aggie's magic.

And now Elizabeth and I are going to die.

Across the room Frank uttered a triumphant roar as he moved in on Elizabeth, his ax blade raised high.

Chapter
29

"Simon—*stop him!*"

Elizabeth's terrified cry rang in Simon's ears.

He started to leap at Frank, hoping to pull him down from behind.

But Simon stopped halfway across the kitchen.

And stared in amazement as the ax fell from Frank's hand, ringing against the stone hearth.

Frank's eyes rolled back in his head. He uttered a startled cry and crumpled to the floor.

Elizabeth's eyes flew open. Her entire body was trembling.

Simon bent over Frank's body and examined him.

Dead. Frank was dead. The poison had worked.

Simon ran to comfort his sister. He wrapped his arms around her and held her until she stopped shaking. "We are safe now," he whispered. "We are both safe."

Elizabeth nodded, crying softly, and buried her head in his chest.

Simon gazed over her shoulder at the gruesome scene in the kitchen. His mother and father lay in congealing pools of blood.

They had always been kind, good people, Simon knew. They were kind and took in a starving drifter— and he murdered them in return.

Kate had never harmed anyone in her life. And she had been brutally, coldly murdered, too.

Goodness is weakness, Simon told himself. *That is clear to me now.*

Goodness is weakness.

Only evil can fight evil.

Elizabeth and I will leave this house, he decided, holding his sister, letting her cry. This house holds only memories of horror for me.

Elizabeth's tears slowed. "Simon," she said, "you saved my life." She touched the silver amulet again. "We are orphans now. You and I are the only ones left alive. I—I cannot help feeling that this amulet had something to do with saving us."

The silver disk flashed in the firelight. The deep blue stones glowed like human eyes.

Elizabeth pulled the pendant over her head. She gazed at it, then held it out to Simon.

"I want you to have it," she said. "Please—take it. Its power saved me. From now on, that power must be yours."

Simon bent forward, and Elizabeth slid the silver chain over his head.

Immediately he felt warm. He closed his eyes, but instead of darkness he saw flames, hot red fire.

The flames faded quickly, and then Simon saw only Elizabeth's tear-stained face, watching him.

He led his sister away from the scene of horror, out of the kitchen, into the cool night air. He thought of the flames, and Old Aggie's words echoed in his mind.

"The letters in your name spell fire—and that is how your family will come to its end. By fire."

I will not let it happen, Simon thought grimly as he and Elizabeth stared at the full moon rising. Old Aggie's prediction will not come true.

I have the power to stop it. I can change the future.

The last Goode is dead, he thought with satisfaction. The feud is over now. The curse has been erased. All except for the fire, the fire in my name . . .

The amulet burned against his chest as he thought about the fire, the letters in his name. And then, suddenly, he knew—he knew exactly what he had to do.

It is simple, he thought. I will change my name.

I will change the letters, so that they will no longer spell *fire*. That will end the curse once and for all.

Elizabeth gripped his hand tightly. She is still afraid, he thought sadly. She does not understand that there is no need to be afraid anymore.

There are no more Goodes. No more feud. No more curse. We are safe. This time, it really is over.

I am the one who can beat the ancient curse. I am powerful. I will change the future, beginning with my name.

I am no longer Simon Fier.

Now and forever I will be known as *Simon FEAR*.

Village of Shadyside
1900

The candle burned low as Nora continued to write. She dreaded the moment when the candle would sputter and die.

But even more she dreaded the dawn.

She glanced at the page she had just written and sighed. If only Simon had been right, she thought. If only it had all stopped right there. Then everything would be different. Perhaps I might even be happy now, living with the man I love. Maybe he would still be alive. . . .

She broke off her thoughts and wiped the tears from her eyes. There is no time for crying now, she told herself. I have much more to write.

The story is far from over.

For now comes the tale of Simon Fear—the most horrifying chapter of all.

About the Author

"Where do you get your ideas?" That's the question that R. L. Stine is asked most often. "I don't know where my ideas come from," he says. "But I do know that I have a lot more scary stories in my mind that I can't wait to write."

So far, R.L. has written nearly three dozen mysteries and thrillers for young people, all of them bestsellers.

R.L. grew up in Columbus, Ohio. Today he lives in an apartment near Central Park in New York City with his wife, Jane, and thirteen-year-old son, Matt.

THE NIGHTMARES
NEVER END ...
WHEN YOU VISIT

Next ...
THE FEAR STREET SAGA:
THE BURNING
(Coming October 1993)

Young Simon falls in love with the beautiful and
wealthy debutante Angelica Pierce—and he'll
do *anything* in his powers to make her his wife.
But then, after moving his family to Shadyside,
Simon discovers that only a precious few will
escape the Fear Mansion's gruesome horror
alive! And so it is left to Nora to tell the truth
and bury the family curse ... before it buries
her!

When the cheers turn to screams...

CHEERLEADERS

The First Evil
75117-4/$3.99

The Second Evil
75118-2/$3.99

The Third Evil
75119-0/$3.99

Available from Archway Paperbacks
Published by Pocket Books